The Curse of the
Romany
Wolves

The Curse of the
Romany
Wolves

By S. Jones Rogan
Pictures by Christian Slade

ALFRED A. KNOPF
New York

THIS IS A BORZOI BOOK PUBLISHED BY ALFRED A. KNOPF

Visit us on the Web! www.randomhouse.com/kids

Educators and librarians, for a variety of teaching tools, visit us at
www.randomhouse.com/teachers

Library of Congress Cataloging-in-Publication Data
Rogan, S. Jones (Sally Jones)
The Curse of the Romany wolves / by S. Jones Rogan;
pictures by Christian Slade. — 1st ed.

p. cm.

Summary: When wolf cubs Donald and Dora, then other villagers, succumb to a strange fever, the brave fox Penhaligon Brush sets out to find a cure, which includes an ingredient found only on the deserted Howling Island.

ISBN 978-0-375-85602-0 (trade) — ISBN 978-0-375-95602-7 (lib. bdg.)

[1. Foxes—Fiction. 2. Wolves—Fiction. 3. Animals—Fiction. 4. Diseases—Fiction. 5. Healers—Fiction. 6. Adventure and adventurers—Fiction.] I. Slade, Christian, ill. II. Title.

PZ7.R625525Cur 2009

[Fic]—dc22   2008040882

The text of this book is set in 12-point Village.

Printed in the United States of America
August 2009
10 9 8 7 6 5 4 3 2 1
First Edition

For Mum,
Thanks for the grandest adventure of all.
—S.J.R.

For Penny & Leo
—C.S.

An Ominous Sky

Penhaligon's whiskers twitched as he sniffed the damp, salty air. The skies beyond Rock Pool Lighthouse were already gray, and gulls squealed shrill warnings as they circled the harbor. Seagulls, he knew, did not need gathering clouds and choppy seas to sense that they must fly to shore, safe from an approaching storm.

He should finish his task promptly and return to Ferball Manor before the squall, but he lingered. For here on Brigand's Point, high above Porthleven Bay, the view was awesome. The craggy headlands stretched into an ocean that heaved up and down as though breathing, where waves flung themselves against the cliffs in foaming white fits. Penhaligon stared seaward, as though his keen fox eyes would see what lay beyond the steely horizon if only he looked hard enough.

A flotilla of fishing boats sailed into view, their rust-colored sails straining in the wind as they headed for safe harbor. Penhaligon recognized Hotchi-witchi's bright blue boat in the lead.

Steady, my old friend, he thought as the fleet clipped almost too close to the Rock Pool cliffs, and past the spare, barnacled ribs of a wrecked ship. Penhaligon buttoned his tweed jacket against the late spring chill.

"Careful what you wish for, Penhaligon Brush," said a laughing voice behind him. He dragged his gaze from the ship's remains. "Hello, Rowan," he said, throwing his polishing cloth onto the grass. He smiled at his fox-mate and brushed back his large ears. Three whole seasons they'd been together, and her rowanberry-colored fur and sweet vixen face made him feel like the luckiest fox alive. "What makes you think I was wishing for anything?" he asked.

Rowan's amber eyes shone as she laughed. "Oh, I've been watching you for weeks. Every day, you polish this sign on the gate even though the brass is already so shiny you can see your snout in it." She peered at her reflection and smoothed the silky fur around her ears. "And every day, you watch Hotchi's fishing boat heading for open water with that wistful look of yours."

"I just enjoy polishing. . . ."

"Penhaligon," she said, giving him a playful tap on his snout, "you're bored! Hankering after more adventure, I wouldn't doubt. Don't forget what happened on your last one." Rowan's smile faded as she looked out at the barnacled shipwreck.

"How could I forget? I see it every day." Penhaligon sighed. "But it *is* very quiet these days." He checked the pocket watch in his waistcoat. "That reminds me, where *are* Donald and Dora?"

"The cubs stayed after school to practice their dance for the Ferball Festival." Rowan smiled again. "I hope you've been practicing too, Penhaligon."

"Do I really have to dress up in that silly costume?" he grumbled.

"Silly? I'll remind you that the Sea Witch plays a very important part in the festival procession, Penhaligon. Besides, you can't dance or sing."

He wrinkled his snout, thinking about the fishy-smelling seaweed costume. He sighed. "Well, there's not much call for our healing talents these days. Hardly any creatures need curing. There hasn't been a customer in the apothecary in weeks, and the only creature in the hospital is there because he won't leave," said Penhaligon.

"Yes," said Rowan, thoughtful all of a sudden. "We really must have a chat with old Bill Goat. He complains of stomachaches but eats us out of house and hospital. I heard that since they moved here from Ramble-on-the-Water, Mrs. Goat spends more time in her flower garden than her kitchen." Rowan placed her paw on Penhaligon's shoulder. "You finish polishing the sign, and I'll make us a nice cup of tea." She raised her muzzle and sniffed the air. "You'd better hurry. There's a storm coming." Rowan picked up her skirts and walked briskly along the rhododendron-lined driveway from whence she came.

"I always thought you liked my singing," muttered Penhaligon as he watched Rowan head toward the stone-built Ferball Manor. The grand manor house on Brigand's Point, with its turreted roof and sweeping ocean views, was now their beautiful home. It was hard to imagine that at one time he'd been held prisoner in the manor's ancient dungeon. Penhaligon grimaced as he thought of his former captor and briefly wondered where the dastardly Sir Derek was now. He grabbed a clean cloth from his basket.

Nowadays, he and Rowan kept the dungeon stocked with pills and potions rather than prisoners. There were plenty of shelves for the neatly labeled bottles and boxes of herbals, all sorted in alphabetical order. They prepared their cures and remedies on a long counter placed in front of the shelves. Each fox had their own stone mortar and pestle for grinding and mixing, but the two shared the shiny brass scales that Penhaligon had inherited from his grandfather Menhenin.

There was a large, roughly carved hole in the dungeon floor that opened onto a craggy, sea-washed cavern beneath Ferball Manor. Lady Ferball's ancestors had once used the sea hole, along with the many secret passages throughout the house, to move treasures "given" to them by the sea. Many of these treasures were washed ashore from unfortunate shipwrecks, dashed against the jagged rocks of Rock Pool Cliff. Unhappily, the ships' owners did not agree that the treasures belonged to Lady Ferball's ancestors, so it was generally thought that keeping them hidden was the best way to avoid an argument.

High tides almost filled the cave, so Penhaligon had made a sturdy wooden cover for the sea hole. This muffled the sound of the crashing waves but did little to keep out the damp air, so the more delicate mixtures and mineral powders were stored in tightly sealed containers. But overall, the cool dungeon temperature worked well. Penhaligon and Rowan had all that was needed for running an apothecary and a hospital, just as old Lady Ferball had requested when she left the manor to them.

Penhaligon breathed in the scent of the chestnut trees that surrounded his home. The rhododendron bushes promised to erupt with scorching-pink flowers, and bluebells the color of a rich Spatavian rug would soon carpet the ground. The fox smiled and glanced at the ocean once more. Rowan was right, as usual. But was there something wrong with wondering what was over the horizon? He gave the sign a final swipe.

LADY FERBALL MEMORIAL HOSPITAL
FOR CREATURES GREAT AND SMALL

Life was good—quiet, but good—and a cup of tea would go down nicely, especially if there was a piece of ginger cake to go with it. He picked up his basket of polishes and cloths.

Just then, he saw Dora racing up the mud-puddled

village track, her skinny wolf-cub legs skidding in all directions.

"Uncle Penhaligon! Uncle Penhaligon! Come quick!" She could barely squeak out the words. "It's Donald. Oh, he's awful ill. Mr. Bancroft has him at the schoolhouse."

"Ill? Donald? He was fine this morning." Penhaligon fixed her with a look. "Is this another get-out-of-homework scheme?"

"No! I promise. . . . Cross my heart and hope to die, no." Dora crossed her body with both paws. "It was all of a sudden. . . . We were halfway through dancing the Porthleven Pipe and it was our turn to dance the reel, and Donald breathed sort of funny, like this"—Dora gasped and gulped for air—"and then, bang! Fell right over in a dead faint." She lay stiff on the muddy ground, her large brown eyes staring at the sky.

"Flaming foxgloves!" said Penhaligon. "Why didn't you say?"

"But . . ."

"Never mind, run and tell Rowan I've gone to see him." Penhaligon hurried down the track toward the village. It wasn't normal for a healthy wolf cub to faint: too much dancing and chocolate, if he knew Donald.

When he'd first met Rowan and the cubs, he had thought it very odd that a vixen should adopt two wild wolf cubs when most creatures feared and despised the Romany wolves, himself included. But then Penhaligon had had to change his opinion when he'd discovered his own dark family secret. Though he looked like his fox mother, his father had been a wolf—a Romany wolf from the Purple Moor. Donald and Dora were indeed wild and found at least ten types of trouble to get into on most days, but he loved them as his own, and they were the closest he'd ever be to the wolf family he'd never known.

Porthleven Harbor was bustling when Penhaligon headed past the clock tower and across the cobblestoned quayside. Villagers were busy stringing banners and bright-colored bunting across the square.

"Not long now, Mr. Penhaligon," called Old Amon from the top of his ladder. "Just two weeks till festival. The young 'uns are lookin' forward to being terrified to the tips of their whiskers by the Sea Witch." He chuckled to himself. "I'll be collectin' the seaweed for yer costume like usual; good and slimy this year, special for ye."

Penhaligon forced half a smile as an unpleasant, fishy smell crept up his nostrils again, even though there was no seaweed to be seen. "Thanks, Amon. Be careful up there on that ladder."

"Oh, aye," said Old Amon. He pointed to the gray clouds boiling above the harbor. "I'll be done before the storm."

The tower clock struck five bells. Penhaligon hurried past the Cat and Fiddle Public House and hardly noticed the merry sounds of fiddles and drums as musicians practiced festival songs between pints of cowslip ale. Nor did he notice the cottage window boxes that overflowed with tumbling crimson chrysanthemums and the hanging baskets bursting forth with begonias of yellow and orange, grown especially for the most coveted prize on festival day—Best Cottage in Bloom.

He hastened on, nodding good-day to Mrs. Goat as she deadheaded her scarlet geraniums. She bleated cheerily and didn't even ask about Bill Goat. It crossed Penhaligon's mind that Rowan was right again, this time about Bill's mysterious stomachaches.

"Ahoy there! Penhaligon!" a spiny hedgehog dressed

in oilskins called from one of the fishing boats now tied up alongside the quay. "Got a nice catch of fresh 'errings. Would ye like some for yer supper?"

"Thanks, Hotchi, but I can't stop. Donald's not well."

The hedgehog grinned. "Trying to get out of 'is 'ome-work again, is 'e? Remember when 'e colored 'is tongue purple with black currants and claimed 'e 'ad the purple plague? Don't ye worry yerself, Penhaligon." Hotchi glanced at the darkening sky. "I'll see ye later. Got to unload before the storm comes, I reckon." He turned back to his herring barrels.

Penhaligon smiled, and felt strangely relieved. Hotchi had known the cubs for even longer than he. They were famous for their ability to find trouble. He slowed his pace a little and turned up a narrow street, away from the hustle and bustle of the quayside.

The schoolhouse—where Penhaligon's badger brother, Bancroft Brock, was head teacher—sat in the quiet of shade trees, next to the bowling green. The school playground was empty, and all the chattering pupils were clambering over each other, trying to look through a crack in the shuttered window. Hannah, Hotchi's daughter and Bancroft's head pupil, hurried out, her hedgehog prickles bristling, to chase them away.

"Go on now, I told all of you! School's over. Shoo—or I'll be issuing lines tomorrow."

"Mr. Penhaligon's come!" someone hissed.

There was a hush so quiet that Penhaligon could hear his own heartbeat. The students watched as he pushed through the small crowd.

"Oh, Mr. Penhaligon. At last!" said Hannah, a look of relief flooding her bright, round eyes. "Quickly. Come inside."

Beyond the rows of wooden desks, near the chalkboard, Bancroft was sitting on the floor, with Donald's furry head cradled in his lap. Penhaligon's heart continued to pound. His stomach felt like stone. He tried to read Bancroft's face. He'd been raised by Bancroft's badger family and knew every expression of his brother's kindly face, but the room was dim. As his eyes grew accustomed to the light, he made out Donald's stiffened body, lying as though the life had been drawn out of it.

"Bancroft!" Penhaligon gasped. "He's not . . . ?"

"Oh, my brother." Bancroft hung his head. "I really don't know."

At that moment, as the first raindrops began to fall, Penhaligon knew that homework was the least of Donald's worries.

The Curse

It was Rowan, with her fox's sharp sense of smell, who had discovered the pustule-like swellings behind Donald's hairy ears. The cub was lying on the crisp white hospital bedsheets, staring at nothing, with a dead creature's eyes. His long, dark fur was wet from the sweat of fever.

Rowan took Penhaligon aside. "I've seen this before," she said in what was almost a whisper. "The high fever, the unblinking stare, the stinking, putrid swellings . . . they start behind the ear. . . ."

Penhaligon nodded. He too recognized this illness. He also knew that soon the poison-filled swellings would cover Donald's paws. But that would not be the worst. It was the pustules they could not see that were the most dangerous, the ones inside his body. Penhaligon dreaded Rowan's next words, but knew he had to listen.

"These are symptoms of the sickness that wiped out the Romany wolves so many seasons ago. I shall never forget that terrible time of despair. We nursed so many, Mennah and I, until she too . . ." Rowan's voice trailed off. She swallowed hard. "You must have seen it, Penhaligon, when Menhenin was ill; he was from the same Purple Moor tribe. It's the Curse. The Curse of the Romany Wolves."

The words echoed around Penhaligon's head. It couldn't be possible. The devastating disease had died out with the wolves. Donald and Dora were the only survivors, and they had always been as healthy as herring gulls.

Penhaligon felt a veil of sadness wrap around his body as he recalled the illness of his grandfather and apothecary teacher, Menhenin. Penhaligon had not been able to save him, though he had attended the old wolf night and day, to the point of exhaustion. No cure had helped. Menhenin himself had been strangely calm, accepting, almost as though he knew his fate.

"Yes, I have seen it," Penhaligon said quietly, "though I did not know at the time what the sickness was."

"How could you have guessed? Menhenin kept his wolf identity secret. You would not have suspected a sickness that affected only wolves. Besides," she added, "there was nothing you could have done. Mennah and I tried everything—studied ancient family cures over and over, until she fell to the sickness herself. Penhaligon, what are we to do?"

He heard the panic in her voice and hoped she couldn't detect the same in his. "Try not to worry. We'll find a cure." He placed his paws around her.

"You know as well as I, Penhaligon: this is wolf fever; there *is* no cure."

Was she right? They *had* all died: Menhenin; his sister wolf, Mennah; the Romany wolves from the moor. Some of the desperate tribe had left, but had never been heard from again. Donald and Dora were the only two spared. But had wolf fever now returned to claim the ones it had left behind?

They heard singing and turned to see Dora sitting on Donald's bed, holding his paw.

"Dora!" Rowan barked. "Get away from him right now!"

"But I want to see Donald. What's wrong with him, and what's that stinky smell?"

Rowan snatched Donald's paw away from her. "Leave this minute!"

"Why are you shouting at me?" Dora shouted back.

"I want to know what's wrong."

"Don't come back until I say so!" Rowan pointed to the door.

Dora's snout quivered with anger. "I hate you!" she growled, and ran from the ward.

Penhaligon watched Rowan's eyes well with tears. "There is no cure for wolf fever," she said again.

"Rowan, I won't give up till we discover one." He hoped his words sounded more confident than he was feeling. "Why don't you rest? We have a long night ahead. I'll watch Donald for a while."

Rowan gave a heavy sigh. "I can't rest, Penhaligon. And we haven't even talked about what will happen if this news gets out. The rumors, the fear and prejudice toward the wolves . . . What about Dora? And you? Remember how long I was an outcast in this village—a vixen, raised by a Romany wolf?"

"Now, Rowan, you worry too much. Creatures have moved on since all that superstitious nonsense. Everyone respects you and loves you and the cubs. So what if Mennah was a wolf? Because of her, you are a talented healer. What's more, through both you and me, the villagers have had benefits from ancient wolf knowledge that they would never have had otherwise. They know there is nothing to fear."

Bill Goat had been watching and listening from his bed at the other end of the ward. He stroked his white beard thoughtfully. "So . . . the Curse of the Romany Wolves returns. Well, good luck to you, Penhaligon," he mumbled as he heaved himself out of his comfy bed and grabbed his walking stick. It was time for him to leave.

The wind-driven rain chittered against the windows. Penhaligon set down his apothecary book to draw the curtains. He had studied dozens of books and his candle had burned down to within a bare inch of the holder, but still he could find nothing regarding wolf fever. It was as though the disease had never existed. How could the books written by great apothecaries of the past fail to mention such a terrible disease? Had the wolves really been so hated that other creatures had simply ignored the illness? He pressed his paws against his aching eyes.

He should check on Donald. Lighting a fresh candle, he started down the sweeping red-carpeted staircase of Ferball Manor. He paused in front of a portrait in a large gold frame. Lady Ferball's feline emerald eyes smiled upon him. The artist had captured the old cat's lively spirit so well that Penhaligon felt he could almost reach out and touch her. "Dear Lady Ferball, how I wish you were here with us right now," he said quietly.

Once downstairs, he crossed the black-and-white-marbled entrance foyer to the hospital ward. The

ward had once been the manor's grand ballroom, and the ceiling was painted with colorful scenes from Ferball family history: tall ships and castles and royal-looking felines captured forever in oil paint. Sometimes Penhaligon would lie on one of the hospital beds just to gaze and imagine.

But now he had eyes only for Rowan and Donald. The vixen sewed as she sang softly to the still, staring cub. She smiled, but Penhaligon could see the rims of her eyes, stung pink from tears.

"I've given Donald an infusion of feverfew tea and have poulticed the swellings behind his ears with bog mud and oat grass." Rowan pointed to the thick layers of brown gunk behind his ears. "He seems more comfortable, but his eyes are so dry from the staring. I bathed them with nettle juice." She tried to sound matter-of-fact, but the edges of her snout trembled a little.

"He knows you're taking the very best care of him," said Penhaligon gently. "What are you sewing?"

Rowan held up a dark blue tunic. She was working on the scarlet embroidery around the neck. "It's Donald's costume . . . for the festival. I feel I must finish it, even though . . ." Her voice trailed off.

"We'll find a cure, Rowan. There must be a cure.

It's just a matter of knowing where to look and what to look for." Penhaligon waved his paw in front of Donald's eyes; they did not even flicker. "Are there any signs of swellings on his paws?" he asked.

"Not yet," said Rowan.

"I remember Menhenin's sickness. . . . After the paw swellings, his fever broke. He felt much better for a while."

"Yes. But then the swellings burst," said Rowan, "and the cough comes." She stabbed the needle into the tunic and fiercely drew the red thread through the fabric.

Both foxes knew that this was when the poison spread inside the body. After that, it would only be a short time before the infected creature lost the battle with wolf fever.

"How did Donald catch such a disease?" asked Rowan.

Penhaligon shook his head. He had been puzzling over the same question. "Has he been anywhere unusual recently? Perhaps he came in contact with something tainted by wolf fever?"

Rowan shrugged. "Not that I know of, but you know they only confess to half their mischief." She smiled and stroked Donald's brow.

"I wonder if they sneaked down the old tin mine again." Penhaligon felt the tips of Donald's ears. "You know how fascinated they are with those damp old tunnels. Goodness knows why." He felt chilled just thinking about the cramped, dark mine. "We need to speak to Dora; they are always together."

Rowan thought for a minute. "That's true, except for the time I sent him to the cliffs at Rock Pool. We needed more snake-egg shells for Bill Goat's stomach-ache cure."

Penhaligon sighed. "Well, unless he met a stray infected wolf over there, I can't see that Rock Pool would be a problem." He scratched his head. "Menhenin taught me that sometimes a disease can live in a creature for a long time, but might only make that creature sick when the disease becomes stronger than its victim."

"Donald? Weak?" Rowan stroked Donald's paw and hummed the sweet yet melancholy melody she had previously been singing.

The tune stirred a sudden swelling of emotion inside Penhaligon. He wasn't sure if it was a feeling of sadness or hope. "That song . . . I recognize it. Menhenin used to sing it sometimes when he was working in the apothecary in Ramble-on-the-Water."

"It's a Romany wolf song," said Rowan, "a lullaby

to soothe aching hearts. It's strange, I hadn't thought of it in a dozen seasons. Mennah sang it to me when I was a cub." She rested her head against Penhaligon's arm. "My heart aches so much, I think that it's breaking."

Penhaligon jumped up with a start. "Flaming foxgloves! Why didn't I think of it before?"

"Whatever's the matter?"

"Menhenin . . . the attic . . . the old apothecary shop. There was a trunk up there, stuffed full of his old things. There were some ancient apothecary books. I can't find any reference to wolf fever in my books, but I bet I would in those. I hope Gertrude didn't throw them away."

"But I thought you'd brought all Menhenin's old books with you to Porthleven?"

"Only the ones we used in the apothecary. The ones in his trunk he never used—'out of date,' he always told me. It's just a hunch, but, Rowan, don't you see? All those seasons ago, Menhenin wanted to keep his identity as a Romany wolf hidden. It stands to reason that he would hide any books that described the afflictions of Romany wolves."

Rowan looked puzzled.

"Wolf fever strikes what kind of creature?" Penhaligon said.

"Well, wolves, of course."

"Exactly. And Menhenin knew that if I found his fever symptoms in an apothecary book, I would discover that he was a wolf, not a fox, underneath all those flowing robes and turbans he wore."

For the first time since Donald had become sick, Penhaligon saw a spark of hope in Rowan's eyes.

"Oh, I do hope you're right. I mean, there must be a record of a cure somewhere. . . . Oh my gosh! Old books!" Rowan suddenly dropped her embroidery.

"Rowan, what is it?"

"I'd forgotten all about it." Rowan's eyes sparkled with excitement.

"Flaming foxgloves! What?"

"Well, Mennah used to speak of an ancient book of cures that had been used by the Romany wolves for generations. The book was lost, or maybe stolen, she thought, at around the time Menhenin left the tribe. When wolf fever appeared, she begged the elders to search for the book. She felt sure they'd discover a record of the cure. But the sickness spread so quickly that the book was never found."

Penhaligon studied her for a long moment. "And you think the book may be in Menhenin's trunk? You think he stole it?"

"No . . . I . . . Yes, it's possible. Not 'stole' it; maybe borrowed it. Would it not make sense that he'd want to teach his grandson as much Romany wolf medicine as he could?"

The question niggling its way into the forefront of Penhaligon's brain finally jumped out of his mouth. "Rowan, if Menhenin knew of a cure for wolf fever, then why didn't he use it when the Romany wolves on the Purple Moor were dying? Why didn't he heal himself?"

Rowan sighed. "You just said yourself, Penhaligon, that perhaps he didn't want to give up his secret identity."

"I don't believe that Menhenin would let the whole of his tribe die if he had the cure. It's a preposterous thought." Penhaligon felt frustration bubble up inside him.

"Perhaps he became too sick too quickly to think reasonably. But there's only one way to find out. You must go to Ramble-on-the-Water," said Rowan.

Penhaligon looked at Donald, and his frustration turned into determination. He took Rowan by the shoulders. "If you are right about the book, then I promise I will find it. And if it contains the cure, I shall concoct it. Am I not a renowned apothecary?" He pecked her on the cheek. "Just make sure that costume is finished in time. Donald will need it for the festival. I'll leave for Ramble-on-the-Water at first light."

Rowan rolled her eyes. "Let's hope you can make it through the doorway, now that your head is so big. You shouldn't make promises you may not be able to keep."

Penhaligon laughed. It was good to have her teasing him again. He would say anything to keep the despair from her eyes. "So I see we finally got rid of Bill Goat," he said.

Rowan noticed Bill's empty bed for the first time.

"Why, the old goat didn't even say good-bye." Her snout suddenly dropped. "Oh no! Penhaligon, you don't suppose he heard?"

"There was never anything wrong with his hearing," said Penhaligon.

"That's all we need." Rowan grimaced.

The Search Begins

A chill dawn was breaking as Penhaligon packed his knapsack with bread and black-berry juice. It would take several hours to walk to Ramble-on-the-Water, and most creatures, save the odd fisherman, were still asleep as he trudged through the village and started up the steep lane to the main road.

Halfway up, he turned, knowing this would be his last clear sight of Porthleven Harbor. The striped light-house stood proudly on its finger of headland, which stretched out to sea. On the other side of the harbor, Brigand's Point reached out beyond Ferball Manor and its surrounding chestnut wood.

"Good-bye," he murmured softly, and ducked into the scented green tunnel of overgrown hedgerows. Skipper-jacks already fluttered above banks of yellow primroses. Last night's storm had passed, and it promised to be a fine spring day. The hedgerows finally thinned out and Penhaligon reached the main road at the top of the lane.

The sun was higher now, and he was removing his tweed jacket when he heard the rumbling wheels of a cart coming from the direction of Sheepwash. Penhaligon could not believe his luck.

"Hello there!" he called. "Good morning, Farmer Pigswiggin. How nice to see you again."

"Why, thnakes alive, if it ain't Penhaligon Brush," said the large pig-boar farmer. He reined his horse to a halt. "You be on the road mighty early. Can I offer you a ride thomwhere?"

"You certainly can. I need to get to Ramble-on-the-Water as quickly as possible."

"Then climb aboard," said the farmer. He shook the reins. "Thpeed up there, Neddy."

Penhaligon smiled fondly to hear Farmer Pigswiggin's lisp once again. The farmer coaxed his horse into a winding meander only moderately faster than before. Penhaligon knew from past experience that this horse had only two speeds: slow and stop. Still, riding in the cart was quicker than walking, just. They chitchatted along the way about the upcoming Ferball Festival, and Farmer Pigswiggin proudly told

Penhaligon that he and Mrs. Pigswiggin planned to enter the duet-singing contest.

Penhaligon smiled at the thought of the tone-deaf farmer in a singing contest, and he managed to put Donald's illness to the back of his mind—until, that is, the distant Purple Moor came into view. This was the barren birthplace of the twins; the homeland of his father's family; the land of wild Romany wolves, who'd lived their mysterious lives away from all other creatures. Despite the warm spring sunshine, Pen-haligon felt a shiver run up his spine.

When Farmer Pigs-wiggin finally pulled up outside the Warren Arms

Public House, he told Penhaligon, "I'll be taking dinner 'ere tonight, in the Warren, before I drive back 'ome. Tho if ye need a lift, come find me before thunthet."

Penhaligon thanked him warmly and waved goodbye. Then he crossed the village green, where the River Ramble wove its lazy path. He stopped on the bridge to throw a pebble into the clear water. The hollow plop of the stone reminded him of the days when he used to dive for coins that Bancroft threw. He always found them, and Bancroft would lose half his pocket money. The badger would joke that Penhaligon should have been an otter, he swam so well. Dear Bancroft. What an excellent big brother he'd been; Penhaligon really should tell him that when he returned to Porthleven.

Penhaligon's former apothecary shop on Cowslip Lane had not changed at all except for the name on the brass sign:

GERTRUDE SHORTBRUSH
APOTHECARY

A bell bounced merrily on its spring as he pushed through the door. It was cool and dark inside, with the blinds drawn to protect the many bottles of pills and potions from sunlight. There was a new set of brass scales on the counter, and Gertrude's mortar and pestle for mixing cures, but everything else was just as he remembered it. And there, hanging high on the wall, was the huge oil painting of his grandfather Menhenin, his beady eyes still following anyone who looked at him. Penhaligon smiled as he remembered grinding the ingredients for his very first cure under the ever-watchful eye of Menhenin. It seemed like such a long time ago.

"Well, hello," said a voice behind him.

Penhaligon turned to see a young vixen, rather chubbier than he remembered, standing in the doorway to the kitchen, an apron tied around her waist and a wooden spoon in her paw.

"Hello, hello, my dear Gertrude! Please excuse the sudden visit, but I have rather important business."

"It's always a pleasure, Penhaligon. This is still your home, you know, should ever you wish to return." She smiled.

"Thank you, Gertrude, I know. You have done such an excellent job. I hear good things about your apothecary skills. Did I interrupt your cooking?"

"Hmmm . . . Well, thanks to you, Penhaligon, there seems to be a tradition of sending boiled sugar candy to the young ones whenever they are sick. It's the only way they'll take their medicine!"

"Ah, yes. Sorry about that, Gertrude."

She laughed again. "I actually enjoy it," she said. "I have some delicious new flavors. Not good for my waistline, though." She patted her stomach. "So how can I help you?"

Penhaligon told her of Donald's illness: that he and Rowan suspected wolf fever, and did she still have the old trunk?

Gertrude slowly untied her apron. "I'm sorry," she said quietly. "Poor Donald. You must both be so worried. I assure you, Penhaligon, the trunk, and anything else I didn't need, is in the attic."

The attic was warm and dry, and the smell of the straw-thatched roof was strong from the heat of the sun. Penhaligon climbed over jumbled storage boxes and pieces of unused furniture until he found Menhenin's dusty old trunk.

He threw open the lid and sneezed as a cloud of dust blew into his face. As Penhaligon searched through the brittle papers and books, he found some old clothes: turbans and robes, which he remembered were Menhenin's favorite. Instantly, Penhaligon's heart was flooded with fond memories. He fingered his mother's silver locket, which he always wore around his neck. But he quickly pushed his feelings back to where they belonged. Donald's cure was the most important thing right now.

Gertrude interrupted his thoughts. "Sorry about the mess in here, Penhaligon. I've been meaning to have a cleanup for ages."

"It's fine, Gertrude. I've found the trunk that I was looking for."

"How is Dora?" Gertrude wiped a paw through the dust and wrinkled her snout.

"So far, she's still healthy. Rowan has been keeping the two of them apart. I suppose we should be thankful that wolf fever only affects wolves. Imagine the epidemic we could have otherwise!"

"I'm sorry it has to affect anyone," said Gertrude. "But do you remember, Penhaligon, that you also were very ill after Menhenin died? At the time, I thought you were simply exhausted, but do you suppose you suffered a form of the disease yourself?"

"A legacy from my wolf family, eh?" Penhaligon growled. "Well, if it was, we shall never know for sure."

"Things don't always turn out the way we'd like, Penhaligon," Gertrude said softly.

Penhaligon sighed. "You're right of course, Gertrude. I suppose I still resent how the truth about my parents was hidden from me."

"Well, Menhenin could hardly announce that you were his half–Romany wolf, half-fox grandson, now could he? There would have been a riot in Ramble-on-the-Water."

Penhaligon smiled. A riot in sleepy Ramble-on-the-Water was hard to imagine. But it was true: creatures feared and resented anything to do with the Romany wolves, and even though Menhenin had been a brilliant apothecary, the village would have turned against him and his grandson, Penhaligon.

"I know it was supposed to be for the best, Gertrude, being adopted by a badger family, and I loved Mrs. Brock as a mother. But I always felt, well, different. And I hated being teased at school."

"It could have been worse, Penhaligon. You could have been adopted by Simon Slimestoat's family."

"Flaming foxgloves, Gertrude!" chortled Penhaligon as he recalled the awful school bully. "You're right. Now, that really would have been a problem."

For the rest of the afternoon, Penhaligon and Gertrude pored through pages and pages of cures but found nothing. After every book and paper had been examined, Gertrude went to make a pot of tea.

They sat in the quiet apothecary. "Not even a clue," Penhaligon sighed. "Rowan was hopeful that Menhenin might have been in possession of an old Romany wolf book of cures. In a way, I'm glad she was wrong."

"How so?" Gertrude looked puzzled.

"Well, it's a long story, but if Menhenin had known the cure for wolf fever, we would have to ask why he didn't use it to save his tribe."

Gertrude nodded. "I see." She lifted her cup to Menhenin's portrait. "Shame he can't talk to us."

"Shame indeed." Penhaligon stared at the painting. It was then that he noticed something in the portrait he had never seen before. Behind Menhenin was a bookshelf. And oddly, the artist had painted only one book on the shelf. It was large, thickly bound, and ornately decorated. The swirling illustrations were hard to make out, but they could have been snakes, or maybe dragons.

"Maybe he *can* give us a clue, Gertrude. That book on the shelf in the painting—I don't have it. And it wasn't in the trunk. Menhenin never gave away his books. I wonder if it's lost somewhere."

Gertrude stared at the painting. "Oh, blithering bats! I've seen it. I *have* it," she said.

"You have? Where?"

"I . . . um . . . Well, the leg fell off my bed when I moved in. And the book was the perfect size to prop it up—my bed, that is—and I always meant to replace it, but it just slipped my mind. Gosh, I'm so sorry, Penhaligon."

"Don't be sorry, Gertrude. I'm just happy you know where it is."

It took no longer than a few minutes to extract the ancient leather-bound book from underneath Gertrude's bed. The pages were almost disintegrated from age, but the illustrations were still beautiful. Penhaligon realized that they were neither snakes nor dragons, but sea serpents, and saw that they were woven throughout the whole text. The drawings of Romany wolves alongside the serpents made

no sense to either of the foxes. There were dia-
grams, perhaps a family tree; illustrations of wolves
harvesting crops; and a map of an island that Penhaligon did not recognize. The words were written
in a language that neither had seen before.

"I'm sure this book must be important. Why else
would Menhenin have included it in his portrait?"

Gertrude nodded. "It seems to tell about the life of
sea serpents. Do they even exist anymore?"

Penhaligon shrugged. "Probably only in sailors' tall
tales."

"There's nothing that looks like a cure for wolf fever—well, not that I can understand." Gertrude sighed.

Penhaligon turned a brittle page and a loose leaf of paper floated down to the floor. He studied the writing.

"Flaming foxgloves, Gertrude! Look! This is written in apothecary language. I can understand it . . . *febra lupi* . . . wolf fever."

"It looks like a translation from this page in the book. Does it list the symptoms?" asked Gertrude, impatient.

Penhaligon read silently. "There's no doubt, Gertrude. Donald has *febra lupi*. And this"—he held up the paper triumphantly—"is the cure. I have to leave for Porthleven immediately."

"But, Penhaligon, wait—the bottom of the page is missing." She pointed to the lower part of the paper, which had disintegrated or maybe had been torn off. "All I can make out is 'a sprinkle of g—.' "

But for the first time, Penhaligon felt that he could actually keep his promise to Rowan. He, Penhaligon Brush, had found the cure. "It can't be that important, Gertrude. You know that most cure recipes start with the main ingredients. It's probably just something to make it taste better." He scratched his furry head.

"What I'm confused about is the first ingredient, stony lunacrop. Look at this illustration. I've never seen such a plant, have you?"

Gertrude shook her head. "Never. And look, it says 'by the light of the moon, to dry the mouth to stone.' What is that supposed to mean?"

Penhaligon shrugged. "Let's search the apothecary. Maybe Menhenin hid some stony lunacrop away somewhere. Shall we look under your bed first?"

🕯 🕯 🕯 🕯

They explored every shelf, drawer, cupboard, and box in the apothecary, and looked everywhere else they could think of. They could not find anything labeled 'stony lunacrop,' or anything even similar. But Penhaligon refused to be daunted.

"If this is a Romany wolf cure, I am sure Rowan will recognize the plant and know where it grows. She may even have some in the dungeon."

Nothing could dampen Penhaligon's enthusiasm as they said their good-byes and Penhaligon set off, armed with the precious cure prescription and the book for Bancroft, who loved to study ancient languages. Maybe he could shed light on this odd relationship between wolves and sea serpents.

The sun was setting as he hurried to the Warren Arms. Farmer Pigswiggin was just climbing onto his cart, and the two of them started the journey home. Penhaligon should have felt happy. He had the cure, and Pigswiggin had finally fallen asleep, his snores more tuneful than his singing had been. Bright scars of lightning sliced the sky above the Purple Moor as Penhaligon struggled with a nagging question. If Menhenin had had a cure, why hadn't he used it to save the Romany wolves?

False Hope?

CHAPTER FOUR

Penhaligon hurried through Porthleven village with the old book tucked safely under his arm. He did not, at first, notice the strange looks from the villagers or the whispers from behind the shutters now being closed against the night.

Last orders had been called at the Cat and Fiddle, and he saw Bill Goat sitting outside, tapping his stick in time to the fiddlers' music. As Penhaligon approached, the fiddlers played more slowly and then more slowly still, until finally their tune slid in discordant octaves down to silence. All eyes stared at Penhaligon.

"Evening, Bill," said Penhaligon, smiling. "How's the stomachache?"

Bill Goat cast his gaze away, sheepish. Penhaligon guessed he had shared his overheard conversation with all who would listen.

Hotchi was checking the mooring lines of his fishing boat alongside the dock. Penhaligon decided it was time to find out what damage Bill's rumors had done.

"Aye, it's not good," Hotchi admitted. "Folk are saying that Donald's been touched by the Curse and that Romany wolves should never have been allowed to live in the village. Is it true, Penhaligon? Is it the Curse?"

"Hotchi, you have been a trusted friend for many seasons. I will not lie to you. It is true that Donald has wolf fever. But I do not understand why the villagers are acting this way. It's not like any of them could catch a disease of wolves."

Hotchi let out a long sigh. "Well, you ain't heard, as you've bin gone all day, but Donald's chum Cedric Otter is not feelin' well."

"And they think it's wolf fever? Flaming foxgloves!" Penhaligon roared with laughter. "That's a good one, Hotchi. What nonsense." Penhaligon patted the crumbling book. "Anyway, everything will be back to normal soon. I have the cure right here. Found it in my old apothecary in Ramble-on-the-Water—well, under Gertrude's bed, actually."

Hotchi looked puzzled.

"I'll explain another time." Penhaligon laughed. "Right now I have to share the good news with Rowan."

He hurried up the track to Ferball Manor, feeling the eyes of folk upon his back. He didn't care. Yes, he had wolf blood in him, but he was a good apothecary whatever kind of blood he had. Hopefully, very soon Donald would be up to his old tricks again and all this would be forgotten. He didn't hear Hotchi call after him.

"I forgot to tell ye, you 'ave guests— Oh, never mind," muttered the hedgehog. Penhaligon was far away, up the track, lost in his cloud of hope.

🪶 🪶 🪶 🪶

"Penhaligon!" Rowan rushed across the marble foyer to greet him. "Thank goodness you're back. Did you find anything?"

"Rowan, I found the cure, I'm sure of it." Penhaligon was jubilant.

"Oh, Penhaligon!" Relief spread over the vixen's face as she threw her paws around him. "You promised you would. I should never have doubted."

"You *doubted* me?" Penhaligon teased, and planted a kiss on her muzzle.

"Welcome home, Sir Penhaligon."

The fox spun around to see the royal felines,

Princess Katrina and Crown Prince Tamar, standing there. "Flaming foxgloves! What brings Your Highnesses to Porthleven, away from the bright lights of the city palace?" Penhaligon clasped Prince Tamar's outstretched paw and shook it heartily. He had almost forgotten the titles of "Sir" and "Lady" that he and Rowan had received for saving Princess Katrina from her wrecked Spatavian ship.

"We have just returned from the princess's homeland in Spatavia," said Prince Tamar. "We arrived in Falmouth this morning on one of her father's ships."

"We were so close and it has been so long since our last visit to Porthleven, we thought we would surprise you," said the princess, giving Penhaligon a hug.

"Besides," said the prince, "Katrina wished to see if her old ship had yet given in to the sea." Tamar lowered his handsome head. "But I am sorry to find that all is not well with Donald. We will continue our journey to the city palace immediately if it is not convenient to stay tonight."

"The wreck still holds its own against the waves and is the home of many happy barnacles, as you no doubt saw on your journey here, Your Highness." Penhaligon bowed to the princess. "And fear not!"

Penhaligon held out Menhenin's book. "It's just a matter of time before Donald will be his old self. Of course you must stay!"

Penhaligon insisted they celebrate the royal visit and Donald's imminent cure with some of Lady Ferball's vintage ginger ale.

"We love the celebrations," said the princess, her thick Spatavian accent rolling from her pink cat's tongue. She chinked her glass with those of Penhaligon, Rowan, and Prince Tamar.

Rowan's eyes glowed with excitement as she happily read the list of herbs and plants needed. "This does not seem at all complicated. Do you have the

stony lunacrop, Penhaligon?" she asked.

"Oh! I thought you'd have some here! I've actually never heard of it, but I know how you keep stores of Romany wolf ingredients," Penhaligon teased. But as soon as he saw Rowan's face, he realized that something was terribly wrong.

"I've never heard of stony lunacrop either, Penhaligon," she said. "So we have the cure, but no main ingredient?"

Penhaligon felt the flush of foolishness. He'd felt so sure that he'd solved the problem. He'd raised everyone's hopes, including his own.

Rowan let the now worthless paper drift to the floor. "Your Highnesses, please excuse me," she managed to say before slipping back into the hospital ward, quietly closing the doors behind her.

"Oh my," said Princess Katrina. "Penhaligon, eez a terrible disappointment. I am so sorry the celebration eez at the end." She placed her glass of ginger ale on the table.

Penhaligon felt a numbness creep over him.

Prince Tamar put a paw on his shoulder. "Don't be too hard on yourself, Penhaligon. Rowan is tired. Things will look better in the morning. Maybe I can even help. I'll send a royal command to every apothecary in the country. Surely someone must have this 'stony lunacrop.' "

"Hmmm," murmured Katrina. "That may not be necessary, my love. Look at this." The royal feline picked up the discarded paper. "This eez an illustration of the plant?"

Penhaligon nodded.

"I know this plant." She screwed up her face into a tight ball of disgust. "I remember it very, very well from when I was a kitten in Spatavia. We called it by another name, though I cannot remember it. I was very, very ill, and I remember the court apothecary, he insisted to my mother and to my father that I have this medicine. Oh my goodness, it was the worst-tasting . . . No . . ." She stopped and shook her paws. "It didn't even taste; it was just very, very dry. It was like eating . . . stones. Ay, ay, ay—every little drop of moisture left a young kitten's mouth. . . . It eez so very disgusting. . . ."

"Yes—but, Katrina," the prince interrupted softly. "Where did your apothecary get it?"

"Oh," said the princess. "That eez easy. It grows on Howling Island."

Shifty Characters

The next morning, Ferball Manor was as busy as a Falmouth fish market. There was no school that day, and Hannah Hotchi-witchi and Bancroft had arrived to visit Donald. They found themselves dodging flustered warthog guards who were unloading and rearranging the royal luggage between two coaches.

"I've never seen so many trunks," whispered Hannah as she watched Princess Katrina direct the task like a military operation, much to the amusement of the prince.

"Penhaligon! Rowan! Whatever is going on?" asked Bancroft.

The fox explained that the princess had recognized the herb needed for Donald's cure, stony lunacrop, as one used by court apothecaries in Spatavia. "I am to sail on the returning Spatavian ship. Bancroft, I could be back with the herb within a few days! Princess Katrina's father ordered his vessel to return as soon as the prince and princess were safely ashore in Falmouth." Penhaligon's ears twitched with excitement. "The ship's captain told Tamar that once the ship is restocked for the voyage home, he will catch the high tide this very evening. I must leave as soon as the coach is ready as they are not expecting an extra passenger."

"*Could* be back?" repeated Bancroft.

Rowan sighed. "There are complications that Penhaligon has not mentioned. Princess Katrina says that the Spatavian apothecaries will not easily give up their own valuable supplies of stony lunacrop, especially if their stocks are low. Apparently, knowing where the herb grows is one thing; harvesting it is quite another. Penhaligon may have to travel to a place called Howling Island, where the herb supposedly grows."

"I won't know anything until I have consulted with the Spatavian apothecaries," said Penhaligon. "If they cannot give me any of their own stony lunacrop, then at least they will tell me how to find it."

Bancroft looked at Rowan. "And you, my dear?"

"I'm staying here," she said. There was sadness in her eyes as she spoke. "Donald needs to be watched.

The princess has graciously decided that the luggage coach should take Penhaligon to Falmouth so that he can catch the ship bound back to Spatavia."

"That's very generous, Your Highness," said Bancroft to Katrina.

Princess Katrina waved her paw. "I am sure I can do without a few gowns just for one day," she said.

Prince Tamar grinned. "Except for the five trunks of gowns already reloaded onto the royal coach, my sweet."

"Tamar, you are impossible to me!" She stamped a hind leg indignantly, but then smiled.

"Is Howling Island a dangerous place, Your Highness?" asked Hannah.

"My father, 'e will explain everything," she said quickly. "I shall write to the king, asking him to make arrangements for our friend Penhaligon."

🕯 🕯 🕯 🕯

Dora made sure that everyone was busy outside before taking her chance to sneak into the hospital ward, where she visited Donald at every opportunity when Rowan wasn't there. She lifted the cover of nettle-soaked gauze from his staring eyes and signed in the language they had used together as young cubs. No one ever heard her. Donald never responded. But Dora knew he could understand. She crept away, just as silently.

Upstairs, Penhaligon packed quickly. He could scarcely believe that his first ocean voyage would be on a grand ship of the royal Spatavian fleet.

He was placing some clean shirts, his furbrush, and several honey-apple bars into his knapsack when Rowan arrived. "Are you packed, Penhaligon?" she asked.

"Almost."

"Then come say good-bye when you're ready to leave. I'll be with Donald."

She turned away, and Penhaligon felt as though his heart were made of lead. He had wanted a little more excitement, a small adventure—that was true; but not this way, not when lives were at stake. And not without Rowan.

Bancroft was waiting downstairs in the foyer. "You can count on me to help Rowan and Donald while you are away." The badger gave Penhaligon a broad hug.

"Thank you, Bancroft. I'm confident I shall be home in a few days. How lucky that Prince Tamar happened to visit and that the princess recognized the stony lunacrop."

"I don't believe in coincidence, as you know, Pen-haligon," Bancroft said.

"Everything happens for a reason, right, Bancroft?" teased Penhaligon. "Well, I will not ask for what rea-son poor Donald is so sick, or why the Curse has sud-denly reappeared after so many seasons."

"Hmph!" the badger snorted.

Penhaligon opened a small cupboard and took out one of two jeweled half-swords. He and Rowan had received the matching pair when they were dubbed Sir Penhaligon and Lady Rowan. He polished the red and blue stones with his sleeve. "Rowan is disap-pointed in me," he said quietly. "I must not let her down again."

"Not you, my brother. She feels useless, that's all; watching Donald waste away, not able to help him."

Penhaligon took a spare pair of britches from his knapsack and rolled them around the sword. He smiled grimly to himself. Rowan had joked that for their next adventure, she wanted her own britches. He'd given her a pair for her birthday. But Rowan would not be coming with him, britches or no britches. He fastened the buckles of his pack.

The royals were ready to leave for the city.

"Eez my father's fastest ship," the princess told Penhaligon. She pulled off her royal ring. "Here! This eez your introduction to the royal court. My father will be honored to finally meet the creature that once saved his daughter's life. He will bestow many gifts upon you." She laughed, as Penhaligon had always refused any reward for his good deed of the past.

"I am in your service, Princess, and need no gift except safe passage to find the herb." Penhaligon bowed.

"Do not worry, Penhaligon. If there eez no stony lunacrop for you at the court, Howling Island eez but a day's sail from Spatavia. My father will organize everything. Just give him this." The princess handed Penhaligon a letter in an envelope stamped with her own royal seal. "It explains everything."

"And this is from me." Prince Tamar placed a purse of gold coins into Penhaligon's paw. "I insist that I help fund your expedition. No arguments," he said as the fox started to object. "I wish I could sail with you on this mission, but I must attend to my duties at the palace. I hope for your speedy and safe return."

Princess Katrina wiped a tear from her green eyes. "We will keep in touch with Rowan. Father, he will tell us when you have arrived at the Spatavian court."

She sniffed delicately. "Penhaligon, I should have told you . . . They're silly stories, I'm sure, meant to scare the young ones. But Howling Island . . . some creatures in my homeland, they say it eez haunted by the terrible wild things."

Penhaligon laughed. "And I expect it was named Howling Island because of bloodcurdling howls in the night?"

"Oh! So you heard already?" The princess seemed surprised.

"Well, just a lucky guess. But I'm sure you're right, Princess. Silly rumors."

"Good luck, and make haste now, Sir Penhaligon," said Tamar as he hugged his friend and kissed Lady Rowan's paw. "You wouldn't want to miss the boat!"

"No chance," laughed Penhaligon.

Rowan and Penhaligon waved until the royal coach disappeared down the driveway with Katrina's handkerchief still waving from the window.

"Penhaligon," said Bancroft, "I have been examining Menhenin's book." He handed over the old tome, now carefully wrapped in linen. "I've copied down some interesting text that I'd like to study, and also the paper with the cure translation, which will help me decipher the language, but I think it would be wise for you to take the book with you. There are maps that may be useful."

"I'll take your advice," said Penhaligon, and he hugged the badger. "Now it's time to say farewell."

Hannah Hotchi-witchi was changing the nettle juice–soaked gauze over Donald's eyes. She stood aside to allow Penhaligon his good-byes. The fox took the cub's paw and held it firmly. He knew there was a chance that Donald might not be alive when he returned. But he also knew that without the stony lunacrop, Donald would have no chance at all.

He drew a sharp breath. "I will not return without the help you need, Donald." Then he kissed the cub's forehead, determined that this was a promise he would keep.

"Don't worry," whispered Hannah. "We'll look after 'im. You just get back quick as you can."

"Have you seen Dora?" asked Penhaligon. "I wanted to say good-bye."

"Haven't seen her," said Hannah. "Maybe she's off playin'? Don't worry, Penhaligon, I'll tell her you said good-bye. Oh, and by the way . . ." Hannah smiled ruefully. " 'Fraid you 'ave Dad as a traveling companion . . . whether you want 'im or not."

Penhaligon looked through the window to see

Hotchi-witchi puffing up the driveway, holding his own large knapsack. "Ahoy there, Penhaligon!" he called. "Don't think about leaving me behind whilst ye goes off on another adventure."

Penhaligon smiled. "Good-bye, Hannah."

He went outside to greet his old friend. "Hotchi, I may not be back for several days. What about Mrs. Hotchi-witchi?"

"She can't wait to be rid o' me for a while. Nice little 'oliday, she says . . . for 'er, that is!"

Penhaligon clapped him on the back and smiled. "Better climb aboard, then," he said, loading the hedgehog's knapsack onto the coach. He saw Rowan standing at the top of the manor steps.

"Promise you'll rest while Hannah is here to help?" he asked.

"I'll rest when you are back safely," she said, and quickly kissed him. Then she returned to the ward without a backward glance.

Penhaligon climbed aboard and the carriage rattled down the driveway. The pink rhododendron buds were bursting, and Penhaligon wondered if he'd see them again before the flowers faded. He looked back, searching out the hospital window. Rowan had not needed to voice her grief. Action was needed now, not words, and it was needed quickly. Was that her waving, or was it just the glinting sunlight playing tricks?

No one noticed the slight jolt of the coach as Dora sprang lightly from behind a rhododendron bush and onto the luggage rack. She waved good-bye from her hiding place amongst Katrina's trunks, though she knew Donald couldn't see her. Again she signed the message that she had signed each time she'd sneaked in to see him: "I will not let the Curse get you."

ًّ ًّ ًّ ًّ

Falmouth Harbor echoed with a deafening, jumbled cacophony of clanking chains and creaking ships' timber. Creatures squeaked and yowled their business as carriages rattled over the cobblestoned quay. The heady fish smell kept gulls patiently perched in the rigging of every ship, although the bravest birds swooped the herring right out of the fish barrels and were chased by howling fishermen.

Penhaligon felt as though he had skipperjacks in his stomach as the coach finally slowed and halted behind an overturned cart on the crowded quay. Hotchi leaned halfway out from the carriage window, looking for the large Spatavian clipper that was to transport him to a foreign land, far away from his home and farther away than he'd even dreamed. "Where's the ship?" he asked the coach driver.

"The Spatavian ship is very large," the driver said as he watched a couple of street traders try to catch the cauliflowers that rolled across the cobbles, away from their upturned cart. "She docks in the deepwater wharf on the other side of the harbor. You can't see it from here."

Hotchi's grin grew wider.

"I'll leave you here if you don't mind, sirs." The

driver pointed to the cart that blocked their path. "The deepwater quay is just a short walk along there." The driver gave them a half bow. "If you don't mind," he added again.

"Of course," said Penhaligon. "We'll find our way, I'm sure."

They unloaded their bags and left the royal coach-man to figure out how to turn his coach around.

"Right, Hotchi," said Penhaligon. "Let's get our-selves settled on a luxurious royal Spatavian clipper." He picked up an escaped cauliflower and threw it to the trader.

Hotchi jabbered excitedly as they passed by eateries and public alehouses busy with an array of creatures dining and dancing, or just plain sleeping. Wafting smells of herb-smoked cheese and fresh bread caused Penhaligon's stomach to rumble as he realized how hungry he was. Every so often, the fox had a feeling that they were being watched, or even followed. But each time he turned around, he saw nothing unusual.

" 'Ere we are, Penhaligon," said Hotchi. He pointed to the sign that stated: DEEPWATER WHARF. "I wonder which one it is."

There were two ships, one at each end of the wharf, both with their gangplanks running down onto the dock. Between them was an open space of water, large enough for another ship.

"I can't make out the Spatavian flag on either of these two," said Hotchi.

Penhaligon had a sinking feeling. He saw an old raccoon sitting on the wharf, chewing on a corncob pipe as he tied his fishing nets.

"Excuse me," said Penhaligon. "Are either of these ships bound for Spatavia?"

"No, m'laddy, 'fraid not. There was a big old Spatavian boat 'ere earlier—a royal charter, in fact. See them sails on the horizon?" Penhaligon and Hotchi nodded. "That be 'er."

Penhaligon's head began to spin. How could they have got it so wrong? "But they were not supposed to sail until this evening!" he exclaimed.

The raccoon shrugged. "Well, I'm s'posing they changed their minds, then, di'n't they."

"Can you tell me if there's another ship sailing for Spatavia soon?"

"Hmm, I doubt that, m'laddy. Not for a few days, at least. But you could ask around."

Penhaligon, thinking furiously, said, "Well, if there are no ships bound for Spatavia, how about Howling Island?"

The raccoon almost choked on his pipe. "Howling Island, did ye say, m'laddy? Now, what would a nice young gentlefox such as yourself be wanting to go to Howling Island for?" The raccoon stared at Penhaligon as though trying to read what was written on his soul.

Penhaligon straightened his jacket. "We have business there."

"No one 'as business there—none that's good, anyhow," muttered the raccoon. "Try the Warped Board Public House. There's usually a few captains desperate enough—I mean willin'—to take on a trip for the right price."

Penhaligon and Hotchi walked in the direction the raccoon had pointed. On the way, they asked the crews of numerous vessels where they were headed, but none were sailing in the direction of Spatavia that day. Anytime Penhaligon mentioned Howling Island, the answer was the same: "Not on yer life!" they'd say.

"Maybe we should try asking again tomorrow," said Hotchi.

"We cannot waste any time," said Penhaligon. "I am not about to give up yet. Not until we have inquired at every ship."

They came to the last ship in the harbor. The *Jagged Claw* was a sorry-looking vessel, with its planks green and barnacled. Sails, stained the color of dried blood, lay in heaps upon the deck, and if the rail had ever been varnished, it wasn't anymore. Sheets and halyards lay in tangled disorder, like a jumble of confused snakes.

"I doubt if anyone could hoist a sail with that mess," muttered Hotchi. "The captain should be flogged, by the signs of this."

But to Penhaligon, the state of the ship showed a captain who needed money. It didn't take long to find him. "Look in the Warped Board," they were told.

They found the Warped Board Public House squeezed between a sailmaker's loft and a chandler's shop. The building seemed to sag in the middle, as though there was not enough room for the whole place. Penhaligon ducked through the low beamed doorway with Hotchi close behind.

"In the corner, over there," growled the landlord when they asked for the captain of the *Jagged Claw*.

Hotchi glanced around the crowded, noisy room as several pairs of inquisitive eyes studied them. "You be sure about this, Penhaligon? I wouldn't trust any o' this lot as far as I could throw 'em. Shifty characters, I'd say."

"We don't have much choice," said Penhaligon, tightening his grip on his knapsack. "This could be Donald's last chance. I don't want to lose any more time. I think that we should head straight for Howling Island. We can collect our own stony lunacrop, as much as we need. Remember, the raccoon said we'd find someone for the right price."

Hotchi let out a low whistle under his breath. "Let me do the talkin', then. I'm more used to dealing with the likes of these than you, if you don't mind me sayin'."

Penhaligon nodded.

They made their way to a dim corner. A silver-gray cat, wearing a crimson silk shirt and a green velvet jacket that had seen better days, sat at a table, his head resting on his empty ale pot. He looked up, barely interested, at the fox and the hedgehog as they stood before him.

"You be the captain of the *Jagged Claw*?" asked Hotchi.

The cat stared at Hotchi through heavy lids, curled the corner of his lip to reveal a sharp tooth, and delicately removed a piece of something he'd previously chewed. Then he looked Penhaligon up and down. "And who eez thees who wants to know?" His words rolled with an accent as heavy as his eyelids.

Penhaligon blurted out, "I am Penhaligon Brush, and this is my friend Hotchi-witchi. I won't beat

around the bush: we need to hire your ship, now, and we'll pay you . . . a lot."

Hotchi sighed.

The cat's lids opened a little wider. "Where to?"

Penhaligon took a deep breath. "Howling Island?"

"Forget eet," said the cat, and closed his eyes altogether.

Penhaligon reached inside his jacket and pulled out Prince Tamar's bag of gold coins. Their weighty jingle caused one of the cat's eyes to open. "And I will collect more riches from the Spatavian court after we have completed our mission. Here is the royal ring from Her Highness, the Princess Katrina, as proof." Penhaligon opened his shirt, revealing the royal ring that dangled from the chain around his neck.

A low vibrating sound gently shook the alehouse table.

Hotchi sighed again.

"When do you want to leave?" asked the cat.

"As soon as possible," said Penhaligon, wondering what was causing the shaking.

The cat opened both eyes and sat up straight. "Elgato Fuurrr . . . raa . . . rriii," he purred, loud enough now to shake the ale pots. "At your service. We sail tonight."

Uncertain Seas

"That cat purrs way too easy," complained Hotchi for the tenth time that evening as they hurried toward the *Jagged Claw.*

Even though Penhaligon's stomach was full of a hearty dinner of turnip soup and cheese, his fur bristled against the damp, chilly breeze. The black water slapped high against the wharf. It was now close to midnight, and he still had the uneasy feeling of being watched. "You worry too much, Hotchi. What's the worst that could happen?"

"They could slit our throats and throw us overboard, that's what could 'appen," said Hotchi.

"That's why we'll visit the Spatavian court *after* we've found the stony lunacrop," said Penhaligon. "They won't harm us for one measly bag of gold when there's the promise of more."

"Don't ye believe it," muttered Hotchi. "That bag

of gold looks awful big when you ain't got none at all."

The hedgehog glanced over his spiny shoulder.

"What are you looking for?" Penhaligon asked.

"Nothin'," sniffed Hotchi. "Are ye sure we shouldn't sail to Spatavia first and ask the king for help, just like the princess told ye?"

"I've made up my mind, Hotchi. The tide is right, and we sail tonight. We'll have this fellow take us to Howling Island and then sail us to Spatavia after we have the herb. The king will provide us with a safer and more comfortable passage back home, I'm sure."

Hotchi grumbled to himself as he scurried along beside Penhaligon.

The *Jagged Claw* was hung with twinkling lanterns, reminding Penhaligon of Micklemas with Rowan and the cubs. He would never feel able to celebrate again if he didn't return in time to save Donald.

The crew of the *Jagged Claw* stopped work to stare at Penhaligon and Hotchi as they walked up the gangplank. There was an assortment of creatures, none of whom looked like they had had a bath in a long time. Many sets of yellow eyes studied their

luggage. Penhaligon wondered if they could smell Prince Tamar's gold right through the bag. Hotchi was right. They would need to watch their backs.

A loud, angry yowl set the crew back to work. Penhaligon saw Elgato shouting orders from the helm. A couple of stoats ran down the gangplank to load some forgotten barrels still sitting on the dockside.

"I sorry for my crew's being so inqueesitive," Elgato called. "They think they are on their vacations, no?" He laughed, with his eyes fixed on Penhaligon's knapsack. "Wait there; I show you to your quarters personally."

Elgato sauntered down to the main deck and led Penhaligon and Hotchi below, through a maze of narrow alleyways.

"I don't like the looks of this," hissed Hotchi as they ducked through timbers black with mold. "We'll be lucky to make it to open water in this tub."

"There eez a problem, Mister 'Otchi?" Elgato smiled, revealing his very white, sharp teeth. They stopped outside a small door, which groaned in protest as the cat heaved it open. "Home, sweet home," he said, and gestured toward the tiny space with two tinier berths. He watched Penhaligon drop his heavy bag on the bunk. A low purr rolled around the cabin.

"There is no problem." Hotchi seethed.

"Then I leave you to make yourself all comfy. Call me if you need aneething . . . any leetle thing." Elgato grinned at Hotchi.

"I don't trust 'im, Penhaligon; not one jot," said Hotchi as soon as Elgato had dragged the door shut.

"Neither do I, Hotchi, but I'm afraid we have to put up with him, for Donald's sake."

"Aye. That's the only reason. For Donald."

Penhaligon frowned at the many-legged insects scurrying across the floor. Hotchi was right. The *Jagged Claw* was just a few planks more than a wreck, but it was the only choice they had.

The two friends found their way back on deck and watched the crew scurry around as the ship was pushed away from the dock. Sails were hoisted, and the *Jagged Claw* drifted out to the channel, where a swift current carried them toward open sea.

Penhaligon watched the bright lights of Falmouth finally grow dim, until only the sounds of the most raucous public houses drifted in hollow echoes across the water.

When the last twinkling light faded from sight, the weary travelers went below. Penhaligon took the half-sword from his bag and tucked it into his bunk.

He hoped he wouldn't need to use it.

"One of us should stay awake, with this band o' cutthroats around," said Hotchi. "You sleep first, Penhaligon."

Penhaligon didn't argue. The lumpy pillow felt like a cloud as he lay down at last to sleep. But five minutes after Hotchi had announced he would keep watch, Penhaligon heard loud snores coming from his berth. He smiled; he would keep the first watch after all.

🕯 🕯 🕯 🕯

Penhaligon woke with a start. He lay in the dark cabin, listening. There was a soft creaking as the *Jagged Claw* rocked gently to and fro. There was the muffled swishing of water against the ship's hull as they sliced through the waves. And there were Hotchi's raspy snores as he lay in a deep sleep. But those were not the noises that had disturbed him. From the cabin floor, by his knapsack, there came a scratching noise. Someone was searching, rummaging through his bag. His heart all but stopped. How could he have fallen asleep knowing that danger could be lurking?

He clutched his sword, fur bristling down his back.

Should he draw his weapon? He didn't want to hurt anyone, but he could not let a creature steal Tamar's gold or Menhenin's precious book. There was a slight movement as whoever it was stood up, followed by the sound of rustling paper—the book, for sure. Penhaligon leaped out of his bunk and jumped on the thief.

"Aaarrgh! Got you!" he shouted.

There was a scream. "Ouch! Uncle Penhaligon, it's me. Ouch! Stop!"

"Dora? Flaming foxgloves! What are you doing here?" He lit the cabin lamp. Dora was standing there, filthy dirty, with the remains of one of Penhaligon's honey-apple bars in her hand.

"I was so hungry. I could smell that you had some food in your bag. I didn't think you'd mind."

"How did you get on board? In fact, how did you get to Falmouth? Does Rowan know where you are?"

Dora shrugged. "I left a note," she said meekly. "I hid amongst the luggage. You should have seen the leap I made onto the back of the coach—and it was moving too!"

Penhaligon frowned.

"I followed you and Hotchi all over and then hid in the barrels on the quayside. I knew they'd be loading them. Like Hotchi does on his fishing boat." She pointed downward, to the bilge. "But they put them down there. It was awful smelly, and they were rocking around so much, I felt sick. But I feel fine now; just hungry," she said with a grin.

"You can't come, Dora. It may be dangerous. Besides, Rowan will be worried to death. What if she doesn't find your note?"

"Don't send me back, Uncle Penhaligon. I promised Donald."

Another broken promise, he thought as he gently led Dora to Elgato's cabin.

🐾 🐾 🐾 🐾

Elgato paced up and down. "No, no, no! Absolutely eemposseeble," he told Penhaligon when asked if they could return to Falmouth. "The wind, she eez not right. The tide, she eez not right either. We would be sitting off Falmouth, waiting for the deep water. Still, eez your money. You want to cancel trip?"

"No." Penhaligon sighed. "We'll carry on." He gave Dora a stern look as she grinned from ear to furry ear. "Let's get you some food, and then it's bed for you, young wolf."

Hotchi was still sound asleep when they returned to the cabin, and Dora managed a few bites of bread

before she too closed her eyes, exhausted. Penhaligon stuffed the heavy bag of gold coins under his shirt and gently shifted Dora to make room for himself in the narrow bunk. Sleeping with an uncomfortable lump of gold pressed against his side was better than no sleep at all, he decided.

The next day, a good stiff breeze filled the sails and the *Jagged Claw* cut through the water, creating white spits of foam. Dora watched, delighted, as dolphins raced alongside the bow. Hotchi did not seem too surprised to see Dora: "Wouldn't have expected any less from a canny pair such as they," he'd said. Now he paced the decks, inspecting the ship's equipment and muttering to himself, shaking his head.

Penhaligon was just thankful to be making such good speed. The billowing sails reminded him of sheets on the washing lines at Ferball Manor. But Rowan, he thought with a smile, would never have allowed sheets as patched and grubby as the sails on the *Jagged Claw.*

Elgato had told him they should sight the Spatavian coast early next morning if the wind kept up, and so Penhaligon settled in a quiet corner on deck and watched the crew go about their business. The rocking ship made him sleepy. He had not slept well, cramped in his bunk with Dora and a bag of gold coins. And so he drifted off into a deep, long-awaited slumber.

The fox awoke to loud shouts. Elgato was yelling orders from the helm. The crew was yelling back, pointing over the side of the ship. The sails hung flat and lifeless. The *Jagged Claw* was stopped dead in the middle of a calm sea.

Hotchi came hurrying to his side. "Penhaligon, it seems we 'ave a problem. The wind dropped, and now we're becalmed. Look over the side."

"Flaming foxgloves!" said Penhaligon. "What is that?"

"Some kind of yellow seaweed, looks like."

The weed grew from a tangled underwater forest. The topmost fronds floated on the surface for as far as the eye could see.

"Come on, Hotchi. Let's see if Elgato knows what's going on."

"Eet eez a problem," Elgato admitted. "This eez the Gassaro Sea. The seaweed of this sea, she eez famous for making trouble."

"Then why did you bring us this way?" demanded Penhaligon.

Elgato shrugged. "You are in a beeg hurry for the fastest way. When the wind eez strong, the weed, she eez no problem. The *Jagged Claw* cuts through, like thees." Elgato sliced his paw through the air. "But if no wind . . . then the weed traps a ship. Like thees." He put his paws to his neck in a strangling gesture.

Hotchi's spines prickled up. "You should 'ave asked us."

"I am still the captain of this ship, Mister 'Otchi. You pay for passage, not to tell me what to do."

"There's no point arguing," said Penhaligon. "We are here and we are stuck. What can we do? That's the question."

"We wait for the wind," said Elgato.

And so they did. The sun beat down. It was too hot to do anything except try to find shade. Penhaligon removed his tweed jacket and unbuttoned his shirt. He stared at the gently waving weed. The water looked cool and inviting. Dora joined him as he looked over the rail. A flash of silver darted through the underwater forest, yanking and pulling the leafy stalks as it went.

"Did you see that?" gasped Dora.

Penhaligon wasn't sure what he saw. "I saw something," he said. "A school of fish, perhaps?"

"I've seen shoals of herring when I've been out on Hotchi's boat. They didn't look anything as big as that," said Dora. She flopped down and fanned herself with her paw. "How long do you think we'll be stuck here?"

"Not too long, I hope," said Penhaligon. "Here, have some water. And find some shade."

There was not a cloud in the wide blue sky. Penhaligon had not seen a seagull for hours. The *Jagged Claw* was perfectly still, suspended, like a bottled ship on a painted sea.

The restless crew argued amongst themselves until a scuffle broke out around the water barrel. They jabbered frantically in a language Penhaligon couldn't understand. Elgato pushed in among them and ordered them to stop. They split up, muttering angrily. Penhaligon knew that when the drinking water ran out, things would get nasty. He thought of home, of the cool rain on his fur, and he wondered how Donald was doing. Flaming foxgloves! When would the wind be back?

It was late afternoon when Penhaligon's whiskers were ruffled by a gentle breeze. The flopping sails began to rustle, just slightly. Elgato heard it too. He quickly shouted orders to his crew. They scurried around, pulling halyards to adjust the sails as the wind picked up. There was a cheer from the crew as the huge sails began to crack and snap into life.

"I don't mind tellin', I thought we were done for," said Hotchi. He wiped his forehead with his kerchief. But then the smile left his face. "Hang on; this ain't right."

The wind should have been pushing them forward, but the only movement the *Jagged Claw* made was in a circle, like the hands of a clock. The crew started to yell again, but this time in fear.

"What's going on, Captain?" demanded Penhaligon.

"Oh, eez nothing," said Elgato. "We're a leetle stuck up in the weed. Around the rudder, eez my guess."

"You mean we can't steer?" asked Hotchi.

"Of course we can steer, Mister 'Otchi. That eez, after one of my crew cuts the weed away. Just a few minutes, you'll see."

Elgato jumped onto a barrel, and his crew gathered to listen as he asked for a volunteer diver. The surly crew broke out into fits of laughter.

"What's so funny, d'you think?" asked Hotchi.

"I have a feeling no one wants to go swimming," answered Penhaligon.

The crew's laughter turned to angry growls and they pointed to the water barrel, shaking their fists.

"They didn't stow enough water, looks like," said Hotchi. "We'll all be powerful thirsty if we stay 'ere much longer." He looked at the sails, filling with wind now. "And if the wind gets much stronger and we ain't movin, he'll 'ave to lower the sails. They're in such a poor state, they'll shred apart."

Elgato pleaded with a river otter crewman. He shook his head firmly, making a slicing gesture across his long neck.

"Captain Furrari!" shouted Hotchi, "Why don't *you* jump in and cut the ship free?"

Elgato scowled at Hotchi. "Mister 'Otchi! I am the *capitán*. I do not do the swimming."

Penhaligon sighed. "I'll go," he announced.

The crew started whispering amongst themselves. They looked at Penhaligon as though he were about to do something very foolish.

"What an excellent idea," said Elgato. "After all, eez you in the beeg hurry, no?" He patted Penhaligon on the back. "I get a rope. By the way, I hope you not think you get cheaper fare for this."

"Wouldn't dream of it," muttered Penhaligon.

"My crew, they will lower the spare anchor over the stern. It eez a long way down to the rudder. Use the chain to guide yourself. And here," Elgato said, tying the rope around Penhaligon's waist, "we pull you out if there eez any leetle problem." Elgato showed his sharp teeth in a broad smile. "I prrr-omise."

"Don't ye bet on it," muttered Hotchi. "I don't like it, Penhaligon. The crew's mighty restless about sommat. What if it's a trick?"

"The trick is keeping one jump ahead of that sneaky cat." Penhaligon removed the bag from his shirt. "Watch the gold, Hotchi. In fact, best hide it, and the book too. Now, where's my sword?"

"Here, Uncle," said Dora, her eyes flashing with excitement. "I knew you'd need it."

"You're one jump ahead of all of us, Dora," he said, smiling.

They watched as the lighter spare anchor was dropped off the ship's stern. Penhaligon climbed down the side of the ship a little way and then jumped into the Gassaro Sea. The water felt deliciously cool after the heat of the sun, and a few seconds later he surfaced and waved to Hotchi and Dora, who were leaning over the ship's rail.

Taking a deep breath, Penhaligon lowered his body underwater. He pulled himself along the chain, down and down. He could not yet see the rudder. The underwater forest surrounded him. It cast an eerie yellow glow through the clear water. He shuddered—this would be a cruel watery grave indeed if he became trapped. "Just like diving for coins," he told himself, careful not to tangle his long hind legs in the weedy stalks. At last he spotted the choked rudder.

He thought he saw a quick movement out of the corner of his eye, but when he turned, there was nothing but waving weed. Penhaligon set to work on the rudder. His sword was sharp and cut cleanly through the stalks, but he could not finish the job on one breath. He rose to the surface.

Dora and Hotchi were frantically waving and shouting, but their words were lost on the wind. They

pointed behind him. Penhaligon
turned but saw nothing. He waved
back.

"Nearly done!" he called, and
dove back under the water. With
just a few more cuts to the stalks,
the *Jagged Claw* jolted forward: she
was free. Penhaligon was pleased
with himself. At least he'd got
this part right. Once the
anchor chain was hauled
up, the *Jagged Claw*
could gather
enough speed
to clear the

clinging weed of the Gassaro Sea. As if Elgato were reading his thoughts, the anchor chain started to rise. Penhaligon let himself float to the surface, enjoying the cool water.

He saw three things when he broke the water's surface.

The first was another ship, fast approaching.

The second was Dora and Hotchi being held by force while the crew cast the end of Penhaligon's safety rope into the sea.

The third was a never-ending silver-scaled neck, thick as a tree, rising out of the water. The huge head on top of the neck had eyes the color of glowing embers, and teeth like a dozen daggers lined its open, drooling purple mouth. It was a sea serpent, and it looked hungry.

The Serpent

Penhaligon had never seen a sea serpent before, and he wished he weren't seeing one now. Somewhere in the distance, he could hear Dora and Hotchi shouting from the stern of the *Jagged Claw,* but he dared not take his eyes from the serpent's large, open mouth.

His time had come.

He thought he'd be more scared when he was finally faced with his own demise. But he felt calm, and noticed how beautiful the creature looked— monstrous, but beautiful. The silvery scales flashed green and blue in the sunlight as the serpent arched its neck. A purple tongue, forked like a snake's, unrolled from its mouth.

The other ship was now close enough for Penhaligon to hear a hollow drumbeat drift across the water, but the vessel was still too far away to save

him. He closed his eyes, saddened to think that Rowan would never know that his last thoughts were of her.

♀ ♀ ♀ ♀

Rowan was angry with herself for not telling Penhaligon how much she would miss him. She hadn't even wished him good luck. Wrapped in grief, she hadn't considered his feelings. Now it was too late. Rowan was only slightly surprised to find Dora's note under Donald's pillow, and realized, again too late, that Dora was feeling as helpless and worried as she. Two of the creatures she loved most had left on a dangerous mission, and the third lay lifeless.

She sat at Donald's bedside, staring through the window. It had stopped raining, and the chestnut trees glistened as the sun pushed through the clouds, lightening the bluebells from dull blue to vibrant violet. She saw Bancroft Brock walking up the driveway. It would be nice to have some company.

"How is he today?" whispered Bancroft once they were settled, sipping a fresh brew of afternoon tea.

"He seems comfortable enough," said Rowan. "The pustules behind his ears are very large." She paused. "But nothing on his paws yet."

Bancroft looked grave. "I've come to tell you,

Rowan, that things do not fare well in the village. Bill Goat has told everyone that the Curse of the Romany Wolves is upon us. I've had villagers telling me that they—well, that they don't want Dora in the school anymore."

Rowan frowned. She'd known it would only be a matter of time before the old resentments surfaced. "Well, there's no fear of that, Bancroft. She's run away with Penhaligon . . . so she can help Donald, the note said."

Bancroft smiled. "How come I'm not surprised?" He took a mouthful of his tea. "She has a mind of her own, that Dora. You must be worried, but I have no doubt she'll look after herself."

"She's a Romany wolf. She was practically born looking after herself. But I am worried," said Rowan; "worried that she may also become ill."

The badger sighed. "There's something else I have to tell you. It's probably nothing, just creatures imagining the worst, but the villagers are worried about their young ones. One of Donald's classmates was kept home from school today. His mother says he has a fever."

Rowan's growl turned into a scornful laugh. "Well, I'm not surprised they blame Donald. They are quick to remember the old ways and slow to learn the new.

But even they must realize that it's called wolf fever for a reason: *only Romany wolves catch it.*"

Bancroft scratched his head. "That's the thing that's been puzzling me, Rowan. How *did* Donald catch it?"

She looked down at Donald and stroked his brow. "I cannot answer that for sure, Bancroft. Donald and Dora are the last two Romany wolves that we know of. Penhaligon thinks that *febra lupi* has been lying dormant, asleep in his body for all this time. But we don't know why it is strong enough to make him sick now."

Bancroft shook his head. "Have you considered that Donald caught it from a creature that was not a wolf?"

Rowan's eyes grew wide. "But that's impossible. It would mean that the disease has learned how to live in other creatures. If that was true, then other creatures could catch it from Donald." Rowan shook her head. "It would be a nightmare, Bancroft. Don't even think it."

"Rowan, I think you'd better come and look at Cedric Otter, just to make sure the nightmare isn't real."

🐾 🐾 🐾 🐾

By the time Hotchi and Dora were released, Hotchi's prickles were almost black with rage. A large rat nursed his shins where Dora had scored a few kicks while she was fighting to pull free.

"How could ye leave Penhaligon like that? And in front of young Dora!" Hotchi shouted at Elgato, his voice quivering.

"I know, I know." Elgato held up his hands in a gesture of surrender. "I sorry the leetle wolf had to see her uncle's meeting with the serpent. I thought perhaps he be lucky and we pull him back on board before eet arrived. The fox, he eez so fast. What a great sweemer he eez . . . was."

Dora burst into tears.

"There, there, now." Hotchi tried to comfort Dora as he glared at Elgato. "So ye knew about the serpent all along?"

"But of course. This eez why my brave crew will not be swimming today. She eez famous, thees serpent, in the Gassaro, like the seaweed. Besides, we would be having beeger problems eef the other sheep had caught us," said Elgato.

Hotchi seethed. "And why is that, then? Maybe they could 'ave 'elped," he said.

"Helped *themselves*, more like," said Elgato, "to anything that eez not nailed down, including your large bag of gold coins. . . ." Elgato couldn't stop his loud, rumbling purr at the mention of gold. "And probably yourself and your young wolf held for ransom. The sheep belongs to the notorious Captain Odiferous Dredge."

" 'Ang on a minute," said Hotchi. "Is this Dredge a ferret, by any chance?"

Elgato nodded. "A very stinky, mean ferret. I lost a friendly leetle card game of Pirate Pontoon, and he did not enjoy my note to say I pay my debts later."

Hotchi groaned. "You owe Dredge money?"

"You know thees Dredge?"

"Oh, I knows 'im, all right. We 'ave to turn the *Jagged Claw* around right now and go back for Penhaligon."

"Sorry, Mister 'Otchi." Elgato signaled to a couple of the crew. "Eet eez the *Jagged Claw* that Dredge eez after, I am thinking. So eet eez faster we take you to Spatavia, Mister 'Otchi. You are lucky I am such an honest creature. I wouldn't want anyone to think I took your gold without earning eet. Take them below," he ordered.

Hotchi and Dora, still protesting, were pushed belowdecks.

Elgato shrugged and looked back at the sea. "Eez a pity," he murmured to himself. "He seemed like a nice fox."

♜ ♜ ♜ ♜

The serpent loomed high above Penhaligon. There was no point in trying to escape. He would be scooped up with one reach of the creature's neck. He thought, briefly, about diving into the forest of weed; perhaps he could hide? But the serpent was probably even swifter underwater, and Penhaligon couldn't hold his breath forever.

Penhaligon's blood turned cold as the serpent lunged at him. He closed his eyes and hoped it would be over quickly. A piercing shriek and the hissing of breath sounded close to his ears. There was a splash, and Penhaligon, his eyes still tightly closed, felt his head covered in something wet and slimy. And then all was quiet.

Penhaligon opened one eye.

The wetness was nothing more than seawater and seaweed. He quickly opened the other eye. The serpent lay nearby, its head and neck floating on the surface of the water, its eyes half closed. It was breathing in sharp gasps. Penhaligon saw an arrow wedged between the silver scales on the soft underside of its neck. The wound oozed a dark liquid. The serpent was moaning in pain.

Penhaligon's instincts told him to swim away, but the apothecary in him could not leave an injured creature, not even one that wanted to eat him.

The sound of the hollow drumbeat from the approaching ship was getting louder. It echoed eerily—*thrump-thrump, thrump-thrump, thrump-thrump*—and the ship was close enough now for Penhaligon to see that it was a galleass, with oars as well as sails. Surely he'd heard those drums somewhere before? The oars dipped in and out of the water in time to the beat as the ship glided across the sea. Had they not seen the serpent? Probably not; otherwise they would be sailing in the opposite direction, as Elgato had done.

He swam to the injured serpent. It writhed and snorted, lashing out with its tail. This would not be easy. Penhaligon was tired. He'd been in the water for a long time, and even though he was a good swimmer, he could not tread water for much longer. His mind raced as he gingerly touched the serpent. He must calm himself, must think clearly. He found himself humming the lullaby that Rowan had sung to comfort Donald. Though Rowan had told him it was a song to help soothe aching hearts, it somehow made him feel full of strength and hope.

And then something odd happened. Still singing, he

grasped the arrow in the serpent's neck and the creature began to calm. It looked at Penhaligon with sad yellow-orange eyes. Penhaligon felt sure it knew he was trying to help, as sure as if the serpent had uttered the words.

The fox took his chance. He tucked his sword in his belt, and still humming, he examined the deep wound. It must have been painful every time the serpent moved. If he could pull out the arrow without leaving the sharp pointed tip inside, the salty seawater would help heal the wound. He grabbed the arrow by the shaft. The serpent let him brace his hind legs against its body as he pulled with all the strength he had left. With a jerk, the arrow came free, yanking out one of the silver scales. The serpent howled in pain. Penhaligon checked the wound again. Good; the arrow had come out cleanly. He snapped the arrow in disgust and stuffed the silvery scale in his pocket.

"There you are," he told the serpent, patting its side. "You'll be more comfortable now." Penhaligon again sensed a feeling; this time it was one of comfort.

The galleass was almost upon them. It was a large craft, its boards painted black, with holes cut out along the sides for the oars. There was something familiar about the figurehead protruding from the bow, but

Penhaligon couldn't quite pinpoint what it was. He heard loud shouts. With horror, Penhaligon saw the crew lined up along the deck, armed with bows and arrows aimed at the serpent . . . and at him.

"Ferrets!" he gasped. They can't have seen me, he thought. In panic, he waved his arms and shouted, "Hey! Wait, don't shoot!" But Penhaligon realized they were going to shoot anyway. He heard the order given.

"Ready . . . aim . . ."

The serpent suddenly reared up and let out a tremendous roar.

"Fire!"

A hail of arrows shot over Penhaligon's head.

Just before the arrows reached their mark, the serpent coiled itself with lightning speed, slipped into the water, and disappeared from sight.

"Aim . . . fire!" came the order again.

Now it was Penhaligon's turn to dive under the water. The arrows swooshed around him in a hailstorm of bubbling anger. Down and down he swam, hiding in the forest of seaweed. He saw a distant glint of silver. The serpent was out of danger, but Penhaligon was almost out of air. If he surfaced, he would be shot at again. But there was no other choice, unless he wanted to drown here in the Gassaro Sea.

Penhaligon pushed toward the sunlight. But the seaweed did not wish to give up a new victim. It wrapped around his hind legs like tentacles, trapping him. Penhaligon battled to free himself, pulling this way and that. He felt his lungs would burst. Bubbles swirled around him in dizzy confusion. The more he struggled, the more tangled he became.

And then he stopped fighting.

It would be easy to let go in the cool water, easy just to relax and rest for a minute. He closed his eyes. But as he pictured Rowan sitting next to Donald's bed, he knew he must not give up. He had made a promise to find the cure and that's exactly what he was going to do. With his last ounce of strength, Penhaligon drew his half-sword and slashed at the weed that encircled his legs. He could barely see what he was doing: the water was dark with shadow from above. With one last thrust he was free. He kicked his way up to the fresh air and to whatever lay ahead.

He broke the surface, gasping great gulps of air. He had made it. The black side of the ship loomed large above him. He heard more shouts, and a rope was thrown over the side. Penhaligon grabbed it and felt himself being pulled up toward the deck. He heaved himself over the rail, landing in an exhausted heap.

A familiar gruff voice said, "Why, lads! Look what we've fished up! I'd recognize this snotty fox anywhere! It's Penhaligon Brush."

It was a voice from the past that Penhaligon thought he would never hear again, a voice that made his fur stand on end. The smell of rotting seagull carcass lingered in the air, and Penhaligon, half drowned and bedraggled, squinted up at the burly ferret in front of him.

"Captain Dredge?"

Old Enemies

Rowan and Bancroft walked to the cottage of Cedric C. Otter. Porthleven was unusually quiet. Just a few fishermen tended to their boats along the quay. They stopped to nod hello, but Rowan could feel their eyes on her back. She drew a sharp breath, feeling the sting of old wounds.

"Are you all right, Rowan?" asked Bancroft. "Do you want to slow down?"

She sighed. "Just disappointed. I can't believe that the old prejudice against the Romany wolves has returned so quickly. I've lived here for many seasons and served the village as best I could, but once again I'm viewed with suspicion because I was raised by a wolf and adopted two wolf cubs."

Bancroft looked grim. "Lady Ferball would not stand for it if she were here, I can tell you."

That much was true. When Lady Ferball had

taken Rowan as her companion, there was much village gossip about how the young vixen had been raised by Romany wolves. But no one would have dared say anything to offend Lady Ferball. Rowan held her head high. She was used to taking care of herself, and Lady Ferball was not here anymore.

Neither was Penhaligon. Where *was* Penhaligon? Would the Spatavian ship have reached port by now? Maybe he was on his way to Howling Island already. And what of Dora, that naughty cub? She told herself that Penhaligon would send word as soon as he could.

They reached the Otter family's neat little cottage with pink-washed walls. The window boxes bloomed with a mass of pink and blue flowers—ready, Rowan guessed, for the Ferball Festival. She found herself wondering who would judge the Best Cottage in Bloom contest if Penhaligon was not home. Everything was such a mess.

Bancroft knocked and they were ushered inside. Chinks of light filtered through the closed shutters. Cedric lay on his bed, miserable, with a wet flannel washcloth on his forehead. Mrs. Otter sat next to him. She wrung her paws as she spoke.

"He's proper poorly, Mistress Rowan. Can you do

anything for him?" She lowered her voice. "Does he have . . . the Curse?"

"Hello, Cedric," said Rowan as she removed the flannel. It was warm from fever. She gently examined the young creature. "I'm sorry you are under the weather," she said, noting his dry, hot nose. His usually silver fur was a dull gray, and stiff from sweat. Rowan's heart sank as she felt the lumps behind his small round ears. But his eyes did not have Donald's unseeing stare. The symptoms were confusing.

"Is he eating or drinking, Mrs. Otter?" Rowan asked.

"A few sips of water, 'tis all," said Mrs. Otter through her sniffles.

"I think we should move Cedric to Ferball Hospital for a few days, just so I can keep an eye on him," said Rowan.

"He's got it, hasn't he? You're just not telling me. Oh, my poor Cedric." Mrs. Otter started to bawl. "Is he going to die?"

"I will be honest with you, Mrs. Otter," said Rowan. "He has similar symptoms to wolf fever, but it would be impossible for Cedric to catch the disease, because obviously he's not a wolf. I really would like him to come to the hospital until we find out what sickness he has and if he could be . . . contagious."

"Oh my!" Mrs. Otter gasped. "What about my other little 'uns? Will they catch it too? Will I lose all of them?" Her sobs became louder. "He can't go to the hospital. Everyone will find out. What will folk think of us? We'll be outcasts. No one will come near us, not once they know we've got . . . the Curse."

"It's for the best, Mrs. Otter. We don't know that he has the Cur . . . I mean, wolf fever. And your family has lived in Porthleven for many, many seasons. You are respected members of the village and have

many friends. You cannot believe they would turn their backs on you in your time of need."

"You, of all creatures, Mistress Rowan, should know the answer to that."

♀ ♀ ♀ ♀

Cedric Otter was moved to Ferball Manor Hospital under a cloak of darkness, but the news spread around Porthleven like oil on a hot herring.

Mrs. Otter was right. No one came to visit. Friends brought food baskets for the family, but left them on the doorstep in the dead of night.

As time went by, Rowan was asked to visit more cottages, and more baskets of food were seen on doorsteps. All the young creatures affected showed the same symptoms as Cedric. Villagers stopped saying good morning and instead eyed each other with suspicion. There were no more musical gatherings outside the Cat and Fiddle. Even the fishermen went about their business, alone.

Bancroft finally had to tell the Hotchi-witchi hoglets to stay home, as no one else would send their young ones to school. He decided that he and Hannah would do more good by helping Rowan; new patients were arriving at the hospital every hour.

"I'm not sure what to make of it, Bancroft," Rowan

said as she prepared yet another bog-mud poultice. Her paws were raw, and stained reddish brown from the mud. "The disease is affecting all creatures, but so far just the young ones. They all have the high fever and the pustules behind the ears, but not the staring eyes, and not one of them fainted like Donald. I wish Penhaligon were here so we could discuss this. I wish I knew where he was . . . and how he was."

"Try not to worry," said Bancroft. "If there's one thing I know about Penhaligon, it's that when he's made a promise, he'll keep it. I've only ever known him to break one promise."

Rowan raised her eyes. "And what was that?" she asked.

"Well, it was when we were schoolcubs in Ramble-on-the-Water. We used to get into fights. Some of the students liked to tease Penhaligon about his dark-tipped fur and his large ears—I'm sure he's told you."

Rowan smiled. She'd heard the stories of their arriving home with bloody snouts, much to the consternation of Mrs. Brock, Bancroft's mother.

"Well," continued Bancroft, "my dear old mum, Violet, made Penhaligon promise not to fight anymore. But one day, when I was fishing in the River Ramble, Simon Slimestoat and his bully friends sneaked up and pushed me into the water. It was so terribly icy-cold, it took my breath away. They wouldn't let me climb out, kept pushing me back. I still remember how scared I was. Then Penhaligon came along."

"He broke his promise?"

"Yes," said Bancroft.

Captain Dredge's grin stretched from one side of his sniffing ferret snout to the other. "Here was I, thinking I was going to have another fruitless day, having missed that dratted sea serpent again." He peered into Penhaligon's face. "But I have a feeling my day will be rewarded after all . . . as soon as I find out why Penhaligon Brush, gentleman fox and famous apothecary, is so far from home and his creature comforts and now stands aboard the *Black Shriek*."

Penhaligon stared at the deck.

"Cat got your tongue? Or should I say, Elgato Furrari got your tongue?"

Penhaligon looked thoughtful. "Hmm . . . no, I was just thinking that the *Black Reek* would be a better name for a stinking ferret ship."

Captain Dredge snatched away Penhaligon's half-sword and narrowed his beady black eyes. "You're lucky you are more valuable to me alive than dead, Penhaligon Brush . . . for now. And don't think you can try any of your tricks." He yelled over his shoulder, "Pig-wiggy! Take this prisoner down to the brig. And if he offers you any candy, don't eat it."

"Aye, Captain!" came a shout. A ginger-colored guinea pig with fur spiked into a patchy Mohawk came running up to Penhaligon. Both his ears were pierced with gold rings, and he gave Penhaligon a fierce look as he roughly grabbed his arm. Even though he was half the size of Penhaligon, Pig-wiggy's claws pinched like an angry crab, and Penhaligon was pushed belowdecks. They were almost at the bottom of the ship, and the stench of foul bilgewater caused Penhaligon's stomach to heave when they came to an area stacked with sacks of raw potatoes and barrels of salt fish.

" 'Fraid I have to lock you in 'ere," said Pig-wiggy as he shoved his prisoner into a wooden cage with iron bars. "Sorry for all the rough stuff. It's not really me, you know? When I signed up for the *Black Shriek*, I didn't realize they was a bunch of pirates. Have to play the part, don't ya?"

"Do you?" asked Penhaligon.

Pig-wiggy grimaced. "Signed up, didn't I? Can't leave till me time's up. Is it true you are an apothecary?"

Penhaligon nodded.

Pig-wiggy pointed at his patchy Mohawk. "I used to 'ave a lovely head of hair," he said. "Now look at it. Got any suggestions?"

"Walnut oil," sighed Penhaligon. "Twice a day."

"Thanks!" said the guinea pig, locking the cage door. "You're a real professional. See ya later—there'll be trouble if Cap'n Dredge thinks I'm chitchatting with a prisoner."

"Tell me before you go," said Penhaligon. "Is there a cat on board, name of Sir Derek?"

Pig-wiggy's Mohawk bobbed back and forth as he chuckled. "Not anymore. I remember 'im; 'e kept telling everyone he was some lord, or suchlike. Spoke with a posh accent. "Galleycat" is what Cap'n called 'im. Made 'im scrub the decks, same as the rest of us. Was 'e a friend of yours?"

"Not exactly. But I knew him once. What happened to him?"

"He jumped ship . . . still owes the cap'n money, I 'eard. Hope for his sake that the cap'n doesn't catch up with 'im. Someone said his old mum died and left 'im a castle somewhere. Maybe he was a lord after all," said Pig-wiggy, thoughtful, as he left Penhaligon alone in his prison.

The beating drum started again, and the ferrets dipped their oars into the water. Penhaligon's stomach rolled with the heaving hull. He steadied himself as best he could by staring out at the horizon from a tiny porthole. The Gassaro Sea was soon behind them, and between the dipping oars he could see the speck of a distant ship the *Jagged Claw*. Clearly, Dredge was determined to pursue Elgato. In his heart, Penhaligon took comfort that he might see Dora and Hotchi again. In his head, he knew that if all three of them were caught, Donald's chance of a cure would be gone.

The *Black Shriek* sliced through rough waters, and Penhaligon noticed a school of dolphins swimming alongside the ship. But as the setting sun bronzed the ocean, he realized that it wasn't a school of dolphins after all. It was the sea serpent, and it was following the ship.

Elgato purred to himself as the morning sea breeze cooled his fur. The *Jagged Claw* had made good speed through the night, and they had not sighted Dredge's ship since last evening's sunset.

Soon they would be hidden along the craggy Spatavian coastline he knew so well. Once he was rid of the hedgehog and the wolf cub and in possession of their gold, he could pay off his crew, most of whom he wouldn't trust with an empty mug of cowslip ale. Peace and quiet was what he needed, far away from everyone, especially those to whom he owed money.

It was late afternoon when they weighed anchor in a deserted Spatavian inlet surrounded by tall palm trees. Hotchi and Dora were brought up from their cabin, and the hedgehog looked in surprise at the palms casting long shadows across the beach.

"Now then, Mister 'Otchi, we are arrived. Hand over your gold and you and your furry leetle companion can leave for the Spatavian court. You can tell them of all your adventures."

"But where is the port? Where are the other ships?" Hotchi looked around anxiously. "I don't even see a town."

"Eez not far," said Elgato. "Walk that way for an hour or so." Elgato smiled and waved vaguely to his right. "Maybe longer, with your short legs."

"That's not the deal," insisted Hotchi. "It be almost dark. I have a young 'un here. We don't know our way. Take us to the main port."

"I sorry, Mister 'Otchi. I prefer eet here, in thees quiet place. Besides, there are people I would rather not be seeing in the port."

"More gambling debts, eh?" Hotchi rasped.

Elgato raised one eyebrow. "Eet eez time you left my ship."

Dora glared at Elgato. "If Donald were here, he'd think of something really wicked to teach you a lesson," she growled.

"And who eez Donald, leettle cub?" Elgato sneered.

"He's my twin brother." Dora's voice trembled a little. "He's very sick and needs a plant that grows on Howling Island to make him better. But you let a monster eat Penhaligon." She scowled as a small tear rolled down her snout. "If we cannot get to Howling Island, Donald will die. I hate you."

"Eet eez true this Donald eez sick, Mister 'Otchi?" Hotchi nodded. "Wolf fever."

"Well, I sorry I cannot help your problems." Elgato

thought for a minute. "I make a deal with you, Mister 'Otchi. I let you stay on my ship this night, free of charge, because I'm a nice guy. We set you ashore in the morning. The king of Spatavia eez very sympathetic. He will probably take you to Howling Island himself."

"Don't suppose there's much point now," said Hotchi miserably. "Penhaligon's dead. I can't believe 'e's gone. What am I to tell Rowan? I was supposed to look after 'im, I was."

Dora wiped her paw roughly across her snout. "Hotchi, we have to find the plant, for Donald's sake. I know Penhaligon would want us to try. There's a map and a drawing of the plant in the special book. I saw it. If *he* won't take us"—she glowered at Elgato— "then we'll find someone who will."

"Of course you will," purred Elgato. "So, would you like to give me the gold now or in the morning?"

As night fell, all was quiet, save for the gently lapping waves. The crew of the *Jagged Claw* fell into a deep sleep after their long journey from Falmouth. Even Hotchi and Dora dozed in their cabin. Unfortunately, the raccoon on watch in the crow's nest was also asleep. He did not notice another ship slip quietly into the bay by the light of dawn. He did not hear the anchor splash into the water. He didn't even hear the boat row alongside. No, he did not wake at all until he heard thumping ferrets' feet charging along the deck of the *Jagged Claw.*

"Attack!" he howled.

But the warning came too late.

Elgato Furrari yowled at his crew as they scrambled over the ship's rail and swam for shore. "Come back here, you cowards! Come back and fight!"

But the order went unheard. The raccoon was the only crew member left on board, and that was only because he couldn't climb down the rigging fast enough to escape.

"Tie 'em up!" yelled Captain Dredge. The ferrets laughed and jeered as they trussed their prisoners together like an oven roast.

"This eez a disgrace," Elgato protested. "Untie me at once!"

"The only disgrace round here, *El Capitán,* is your ship." Dredge looked about the deck of the *Jagged Claw* and smirked. "Even ferrets keep their vessels more shipshape than this."

"At least I do not steal like a ferret pirate."

"Is that right? Well then, where's my money? Seems to me when you don't pay what you owe, then sneaks off in the middle of the night, that's the same as stealing."

"But I left a note . . ."

"Silence!" Dredge screeched. He peered at Hotchi. "Haven't I seen your spiny little face before? Let me think, now . . . Porthleven, that's it. And you . . ." He turned to Dora. "I remember you. A real mischiefmaker, you and your brother."

Dora curled up her snout and growled.

"Well now," continued Dredge. "It's quite a reunion, isn't it? Shame I'm not in the mood for a party."

The ferrets laughed. "Let's chuck 'em overboard and take the ship, Cap'n!" shouted one of them.

Dredge smiled and set his dark eyes on Hotchi. "Maybe we should, at that. Tie 'em to the spare anchor and throw 'em over the side!" he barked.

Hotchi quivered. He'd made his living as a fisherman for many seasons, and regretted that he'd never learned to swim. Not that it would make much difference now, he thought as the ferrets hustled them to the heap of heavy chain piled on the deck. Dora howled and snapped at her laughing captors.

"You've played your last game of cards, Elgato." Dredge laughed.

"No! Wait!" Elgato lowered his voice. He started to purr. "Let's talk about a deal . . . just you and me."

"What makes you think I would waste my time talkin' to a cheat?"

"Because I can promise you the gold, *Capitán* Dredge. Much more gold than eez the leetle sum I am owing you."

"This better not be a trick," the ferret snarled.

"Trust me." Elgato smiled his most charming smile.

Dredge narrowed his eyes. "I still have a score to settle with the last cat who told me that."

🕯 🕯 🕯 🕯

Penhaligon had watched from his porthole as Dredge's crew captured the *Jagged Claw*. Hotchi and Dora were now as helpless as he. What a mess he'd made of things. Hotchi had been right: they should never have set sail with Elgato Furrari. He watched the two captains disappear belowdecks. Goodness knew what kind of deal Elgato was proposing. Penhaligon rattled the cage door with all his strength. "Flaming foxgloves!" he howled. "Let me out!" But no one heard.

♟ ♟ ♟ ♟

Rowan woke to the sound of someone pounding on the door. She scolded herself when she realized that she had fallen asleep in her chair. She pulled her shawl about her. The pounding continued as she hurried past the sleeping young ones and snatched a lantern from the table.

"I'm coming, I'm coming!" she called. She pulled open the heavy door and her jaw dropped in surprise. Several of the villagers, including Bill Goat, stood on the stone steps.

"What do you want at this time of night? Is someone sick?" Rowan demanded.

"Mistress Rowan," said Bill, "we're here to ask . . ." A village weasel gave him a shove. "We want to know what's going on." Bill looked down at his hooves.

"Maybe I should ask you the same question, Bill," said Rowan, "seeing as

you left the hospital in such a hurry, without so much
as a good-bye or an 'I feel better now; thank you.' "

"Now then, Mistress Rowan," said a weasel.
"You've told folk this isn't the Curse,
but Bill Goat here heard you
and Penhaligon saying that
young Donald has it. Now
our young 'uns are sick."

Bill Goat coughed nervously as he received another shove. "And we want to know where Penhaligon has gone," he bleated.

"Has he left 'cause he's afraid of catching it too? It be no secret he 'as the wolf in 'im!" shouted a stoat.

"We want answers," demanded another. "How many more of our young 'uns are going to get sick? They caught it from the wolf, Donald. Stands to reason. It's the Romany wolf's fault."

Rowan felt a flush of heat rise to her neck, and her hackles stood up. "Bill Goat!" she snapped. "You see what happens when you spread rumors? And how could any of you think such things about Penhaligon? Who was it that came to our aid when we were starving and the village was under siege? Who was it that helped build the new schoolhouse and turn Ferball Manor into a hospital? Who was it that has looked after you all, day and night, when you and your families were sick?

"It's no one's fault," continued Rowan angrily. "Donald didn't ask to be ill. He could have caught his sickness from anywhere. Maybe even from one of you." She glared at Bill Goat.

Rowan scanned the group in front of her. How ungrateful and selfish could creatures be? She felt an angry howl rising, but she took a deep breath to calm herself. She held her weary head high. "For your information, Penhaligon has gone in search of a special herb needed for a cure. He will be back any day. Now I suggest you all leave and let me get on with my job."

The villagers muttered amongst themselves as Bancroft appeared at the door, having just left his studying.

"What's all this?" he demanded. "What are you doing here at this time of night, worrying Mistress Rowan? Don't you know she's up all hours, nursing your young ones? You should be ashamed of yourselves."

"Everyone knows the Romany wolves were wiped out by the Curse!" shouted a stoat. "I'm not waiting for my little 'uns to get sick and die. I'll leave Porthleven. I got relatives near Falmouth. I'll go there."

Bancroft saw the flash of panic on Rowan's face.

"No!" she said. "You mustn't."

"I'll go if I want," said the stoat. "You can't stop me."

"But don't you see," said Rowan, "if the sickness, whatever it is, is contagious, it could spread to your relatives' young ones, and then others might catch it from them. We all need to stay here in Porthleven until we can find the proper cure. Wait until Penhaligon comes back, please."

"We could all be dead by then," whined Bill Goat.

"Everyone needs to calm down and go home to their beds," said Bancroft. "No one is going to die. Tomorrow we'll hold a meeting in the schoolhouse and discuss what's best for everyone. You'll get all your answers then."

Rowan and Bancroft watched until the last villager had disappeared down the driveway of Ferball Manor. Rowan wiped her forehead with her apron.

"Are you feeling unwell, Rowan?" Bancroft asked.

"I'm fine, Bancroft." Rowan shut the door against the unfriendly night. "Come, I must check on the patients. Did you find anything of help in your notes from Menhenin's book?"

Bancroft stroked his chin thoughtfully as he followed Rowan to the ward. He had been working for several hours, translating the strange language he'd copied from the text. "Nothing that I can make sense of, I'm afraid. It refers several times to sea serpents, and you'll remember that the illustrations in Menhenin's book showed many of those creatures, rendered in much intricate detail. I would suspect that at one time, the Romany wolves had an important relationship with the sea creatures. Do you remember any stories or legends from when you were with the Purple Moor tribe?"

But Rowan never answered. She gasped. The light of her lantern cast eerie shadows amongst the Ferball ancestors painted on the ceiling.

"Bancroft," said Rowan, her eyes wide. "Look at Donald."

♆ ♆ ♆ ♆

Dredge sat in Elgato's cabin with his boots resting on the dining table. "If you are lying to me, Elgato," said Captain Dredge, "you'll be the sorriest cat that ever lived."

"I hear them talk, I see the gold. Eez all jingling and shiny in a bag. I prrromise you," purred Elgato. "You can have eet all if you let me go."

"Why didn't you take it for yourself after you deserted Penhaligon in the Gassaro?"

Elgato looked hurt. "I am not a common thief," he sniffed. "Besides, leaving the fox eez a mistake. My crew, they are panicking. They were supposed to pull the rope, not let go. The fox told me he was to veezit the Spatavian court to receive many treasures after I had sailed him to that creepy Howling Island."

"Howling Island?" Dredge growled at Elgato. "For what purpose?"

"The fox, he wants some plant from Howling Island to cure the leetle wolf's brother."

"Why should the king reward Penhaligon for that? Are you lying to me?" Dredge took a step toward Elgato.

"No, no . . . he showed me a ring from the princess. I speak the truth. The king owes him great reeches for some good deed or other. Eez a shame he became the serpent snack—we could have been very, very reech." Elgato's wide smile showed all his teeth. "So can I go now?"

Dredge stroked the wiry fur on his chin. "It begins to make sense—a reward for his rescue of the Princess Katrina. And he has the royal ring, you say?"

"On a chain about his neck. Why a fox had such jewelry is a mystery to a feline such as myself. But anyway, now eet eez all in the serpent's tummy."

"No, Elgato. Now it is all sitting in the brig aboard the *Black Shriek*."

Elgato's eyes opened wide and he screwed up his nose. "Eet must be a terrible mess after the serpent eez chewing it."

Dredge sighed. "The fox is alive, you imbecile."

"Ah! I was right. He eez a fast sweemer." Elgato sounded quite relieved.

"Right, then. . . . Listen up, Elgato. Here's my plan. I will accompany the fox to the Spatavian court so he can collect his reward while you hold the hedgehog and the cub hostage. Only we don't exactly tell Penhaligon that. Not yet, anyway. When I return, we'll split the bounty, seventy-thirty!" growled Dredge.

"Fifty-fifty!" countered Elgato.

"Sixty-forty!" snarled Dredge.

"Why you get the big share? Eez me who found the fox."

"And then you lost him." Dredge's laugh hacked up from his stomach. "You owe me anyway. Take it or leave it."

"Eez best I get?" Elgato called as Dredge strode from the cabin.

Dredge didn't answer.

"What happens to the fox and his friends afterward?"

"Do you care?" snarled Dredge as he slammed the door.

🕯 🕯 🕯 🕯

Back on board the *Black Shriek*, Dredge ordered Pigwiggy to bring Penhaligon from the brig.

"Seems you have been keeping things to yourself, *Sir* Penhaligon," said Dredge as Pig-wiggy shoved the fox into the captain's cabin. "Seems you have an invitation to the Spatavian court. I had no idea you were such an important creature. You must forgive me for being so impolite."

"What are you up to, Dredge?" asked Penhaligon.

"Why, nothing! I'm simply here to offer my services to you and your companions." Dredge's snout turned up a little at the edges in what Penhaligon took to be a smile. "And to show there's no hard feelings, here's your weapon." He handed Penhaligon his half-sword.

The fox was surprised to see all the jewels still in the hilt. "I don't trust you, Dredge. You are a mercenary and work only for money."

"Ah! This is true, Penhaligon. And I'm sure even you would reward my services after I accompany you safely to the Spatavian court. I'll even deliver you all back to Falmouth with everything you need to cure the little wolf." Dredge's eyebrows almost knotted up as he tried to look sincere. "We'll leave for the Spatavian court immediately for your audience with the king. I hear he is most grateful to you for saving his daughter. That really was such a wicked deed that Sir

Derek plotted that time in Porthleven."

Penhaligon almost laughed. "Oh, and you didn't have anything to do with the wrecking of the Spatavian ship?"

"Just following orders, Penhaligon; as you pointed out . . . I am a mercenary," said Dredge.

"So where is Sir Derek these days?" asked Penhaligon. "I heard you had him working off his debts."

Dredge gave a little growl. "Seems Mummy left him a nice little castle by the sea, somewhere up north of your homeland. He left without even saying good-bye—in the middle of the night. But I'll catch up with him again one day. Ferrets never forget."

Penhaligon slowed the thoughts whirling through his mind. Any plan of Dredge's would surely end badly no matter how good it sounded. Then the seed of a plan of his own started to sprout. Above all else, he needed speed. Donald's life depended on how quickly he could get to Howling Island and return with the stony lunacrop. Dredge's ship, the *Black Shriek*, was fast—faster than the *Jagged Claw* and faster than trying to seek help from the king of Spatavia. His plan was only half a plan. Could he stay one jump ahead? Was it worth the risk?

"I'll pay you to take me to Howling Island,"

Penhaligon finally announced. "And then we'll talk more about my visit to the king."

"But you *must* go the Spatavian Court first," insisted Dredge.

"No," said Penhaligon firmly. "I *must* travel to Howling Island first, and if you expect me to pay you, Dredge, then I believe that I am the one to give the orders."

Dredge's eyes glinted, dangerous as black ice.

Penhaligon knew he'd won the first round.

"Then we shall sail to Howling Island . . . *all* of us," growled Dredge.

♆ ♆ ♆ ♆

"But I have no crew," said Elgato when Dredge told him of the new arrangement. "And I do not wish to go to that island after all. Eez haunted."

"My ferrets will sail the *Jagged Claw* to Howling Island, Elgato. Your ship is mine anyway—until you pay off your debt."

"But I thought we had an agreement."

Dredge growled.

Elgato sighed.

It was a day's fair-weather sail to Howling Island. Elgato had to admit, as they left the coastline of

Spatavia behind, that a skeleton crew of ferrets and Pig-wiggy manned the decks of the *Jagged Claw* more ably than his ship rats. The grubby sails were full and fast. The crew sang as they worked, shouting to their shipmates as the two vessels sailed side by side. All was fine as long as Elgato made sure to stand upwind of the pungent ferret smell.

The cat had, by this time, told Hotchi and Dora that not only should they be grateful that he, Elgato, had saved them from a watery grave, but that he, on learning about Penhaligon's miraculous rescue, had convinced Dredge to set Penhaligon free and they would meet up as soon as they arrived at their destination.

Hotchi was not convinced that Elgato had as much to do with Penhaligon's freedom as he claimed, but he was overjoyed to hear that the fox was alive.

Dora jumped up and down on the deck of the *Jagged Claw*, wild with excitement. She waved frantically at Penhaligon, aboard the *Black Shriek*. She had not dared to believe that he was really alive until she'd seen him with her own eyes. The warm breeze tousled her fur as the ships sliced through the clear waters. They were on their way to Howling Island. Donald would be saved. This was more like the adventure she'd had in mind.

They first sighted the lonely isle in the late afternoon, and Penhaligon was amazed by Howling Island's thick green overcoat of trees that stretched down to the water's edge. There was a mountain range at the distant end of the isle, with a three-peaked ridge rising through paper-thin clouds. The ridge seemed vaguely familiar, but Penhaligon did not have time to give it much thought as warning shouts from the crew caught his attention. He looked over the side of the ship and saw reefs of razor-sharp coral lurking dangerously close to the water's surface. The sails were quickly lowered, oars brought in and anchors let go as the crews moored the two ships close together.

The breeze dropped suddenly. There were no seabirds in the sky; even the ocean surrounding the island seemed still. It was as though time had stopped. Penhaligon felt strangely on edge. He waved to Dora, who, being too far away to shout, signed with her paws, but way too fast for Penhaligon to understand. His signing was rusty, but he would always recognize the first sign Rowan made him learn, seasons ago, before the young cubs started to talk. "I love you too," he signed back.

Tiny yellow and orange fish darted through the water, keeping close to their coral homes. They

reminded Penhaligon of the colored glass bottles arranged on the shelves of his apothecary. His heart clenched with a sudden longing for Rowan. And what of Donald?

The fish suddenly darted away, frightened. Penhaligon saw a massive shadowy body snaking slowly through the coral toward him. The ferret crew was busy on the starboard side, readying one the ship's wooden rowboats. He watched the sleek, lurking body.

The sea serpent silently rose from the water. Penhaligon caught his breath. The silver scales shone brilliantly in the sunshine. It was no wonder the creature was such a prize for Dredge. He felt for the thin scale in his pocket . . . it was still there.

"Go away!" whispered Penhaligon. "Dredge will kill you."

The serpent simply stared at Penhaligon with its

fiery eyes. The tune of the Romany lullaby popped into the fox's mind once again, along with a sudden picture of Brigand's Point, with Ferball Manor nestled in its chestnut wood. Strangely, the view was from low in the water, as though he were swimming in the bay and looking onto the shore. Penhaligon was certain he'd never swum out that far, so how could he see this view in his head? It was as though the thought had placed itself inside his mind all on its own.

"Most extraordinary," Penhaligon muttered to himself. He thought of Rowan again. How worried she must be, not knowing when they would be returning, or even whether they were dead or alive. He fingered the princess's ring. If only there were a way to get a message back home to let Rowan know they were all right. Well, mostly all right. The serpent was still staring at him, and once more the view of Brigand's Point popped into his mind. "Are you putting thoughts into my head?" he whispered.

The ferrets launched the rowboat with a splash.

"Penhaligon!" Dredge shouted. "Let's go. We're ready."

The serpent watched, motionless, as though waiting for something. For reasons Penhaligon could not explain, even to himself, he removed Princess

Katrina's ring from his chain and threw it. The creature opened its huge jaws, caught the ring, and sank beneath the water.

"We don't have much daylight left," said Dredge. "What are you looking at?" He strode over to Penhaligon and bent over the rail. He would have seen the glinting silver tail disappear through the reef, but at just that moment, he was distracted as Penhaligon found out how the island had earned its name.

A piercing, heart-stopping howl drifted across the water; a howl so petrifying it was enough to make a creature's blood turn to cold stone.

Penhaligon's body stiffened and his hackles rose. The howl was terrifying and yet strangely . . . familiar. He noticed Dora on the deck of the *Jagged Claw*, ears pricked and tail swishing furiously. She stood calmly. The ferrets, however, ran around, squawking in terrified chaos.

"Quiet down now!" shouted Dredge. "It's only a wild creature on the island. You're acting like a bunch of namby-pamby school kits."

But the ferrets flung themselves flat on the deck, below the ship's rail, as though a raid of wailing banshees would soon follow the sound.

Dredge drew his sword and held it high. "Get up!" he yelled.

And they did.

"Now then. I need two volunteers," he said.

No one stepped forward.

"All right," snarled Dredge. He pointed to two quivering ferrets with the point of his sword. "Alfred and Bert. Get to the boat."

"Why's it always us . . . ?" Alfred started to protest.

"Now!"

"Aye, Cap'n," said Bert. He whispered to Alfred, "Come on, maybe we'll get paid extra. That howl was just a wild animal, like the cap'n said."

"That's what I'm afraid of," said Alfred. ·

"Just don't fall asleep like you did last time you was given something important to do."

"Won't sleep for a week after hearing that," grumbled Alfred as they climbed down the ratlines of rope netting to the rowboat.

"Get on with it, and stop moaning," growled Dredge as he and Penhaligon descended after them.

Alfred spied Elgato and Hotchi waiting in their rowboat alongside the *Jagged Claw*. His squinty ferret eyes lit up. "Oh look! You don't need me after all!" he said, ready to climb back aboard the *Black Shriek*.

Dredge sighed. "Get back here, you coward. You are the crew, you dimwit. You row the boats! Now *row* over to the *Jagged Claw*, climb into Elgato's boat, and *row* it to the island."

Alfred was about to ask if he could row the boat

he was in, as he'd rowed it before, but after seeing Dredge's scowl, he kept his snout shut. He muttered as they glided toward the *Jagged Claw*.

Penhaligon sat in silence. He had been considering whether he should try to retrieve Menhenin's book and take it to the island. He decided it was safer to leave it wherever Hotchi had hidden it, along with the gold. Besides, the illustration of the stony lunacrop was etched into his mind. He would recognize the plant instantly. However, all thoughts of stony lunacrop disappeared when he saw that Pig-wiggy was trying to comfort Dora. She was leaning over the rail of the *Jagged Claw*, sobbing.

"Penhaligon," she shouted tearfully. "Elgato says I have to stay here with Pig-wiggy."

"Eez for her own good," said Elgato. "The monster eez howling. It is not safe for a leetle wolf cub. What dangers lie awaiting for us? And besides, she eez not well. Right, Mister 'Otchi?"

Hotchi nodded. "You might want to take a look at 'er when we gets back," he told Penhaligon quietly.

Penhaligon felt a sudden uncomfortable knot in his stomach. He hoped Dora was only suffering from a case of seasickness, although he knew that usually she was a good sailor. He called to Pig-wiggy, "Look after her, please!"

"But, Penhaligon!" cried Dora. "It's my adventure too. You can't go without me."

Penhaligon listened to Dora's cries turn into a tirade of angry comments and threats of itching powder in everyone's britches. At that he smiled. If she was planning tricks, she couldn't be that unwell. He raised his paw in a wave.

Bert and Alfred navigated their way through the coral banks, cringing as Dredge yelled each time either of the boats scraped the bottom. Everyone was thankful once the boats were safely pulled onto the white shale beach. They each grabbed a water canteen and rations: dried fish and a loaf of stale bread.

"I'm glad to see ye, Penhaligon," said Hotchi quietly. "I thought you was gone for sure by the look of that sea serpent." Hotchi sniffed at the fish and turned up his nose. "Nothing like the nice fresh 'errings I catch, are they?"

Penhaligon smiled. "I'm glad to finally be here, Hotchi, but I think we'll both be happier when we're home."

They followed Dredge and Elgato across the warm sands while Bert and Alfred lagged behind, weighed down with equipment. The sandy beach ended abruptly at a wall of thick green forest tangled with thorny undergrowth. There was no obvious path, and any route they chose into the dark, gloomy thicket was going to be a battle.

"Crikey!" Bert whispered to Alfred. "I hope they don't expect us to cut through this lot."

"So, Sir Penhaligon," said Dredge with a sneer. "Where are we headed?"

Penhaligon had no clue, but he was not about to let Dredge know that. He had an uneasy feeling that the ferret was working on a new counterplan that would not bode well for either him or Hotchi. He looked at the dense forest, his heart sinking like the sun on the horizon. How far could they possibly get before nightfall?

"Well?" snapped Dredge.

Penhaligon ignored him, deep in thought. If the plant grew by the light of the moon, as he'd read in the cure recipe, then he'd find it in open space where the light could penetrate the forest. He looked to the distant mountain ridge. It could mean several hours' walk but some instinct told him that was the way they should be headed.

"We go that way," he said, and strode toward a small break in the trees.

They walked in single file, pushing and cutting through the overgrown vegetation. Above them, the canopy of leafy green was shot with crystals of struggling daylight that gave the forest an eerie glow. Vines were coiled, snakelike, around the broad tree trunks, twisting up in search of sun.

Hotchi strained his neck, his eyes wide. "I've never seen trees tall as these," he whispered. "Not even in the old forest by Sheepwash. And it smells funny around 'ere."

"I think it's these plants," said Penhaligon, sniffing a brightly colored flower that clung, by wiry roots, to the bark of a tree. "I wish I had time to collect some specimens. I would like to bet there's a wealth of cures across this forest floor alone." He looked over his shoulder into the dense forest. "I don't hear so much as the chirp of a cricket. It's very odd."

"Maybe the howling things eat the crickets, eh, Mister 'Otchi?" Elgato laughed, but Penhaligon noticed that he hadn't been purring of late.

The mere mention of howling was enough to curb everyone's tongue. They walked in silence in the fading light.

"Halt!" ordered Dredge. "Take a drink. We'll rest here for a few minutes."

Bert and Alfred dropped their loads with a clatter and a sigh.

"Shh!" snapped Dredge. "You two make enough noise to wake the dead."

The hackles on Penhaligon's back began to prickle. He peered again into the hazy gloom of surrounding trees. He saw nothing.

The others sat down to rest. Couldn't they sense it, he wondered—the feeling that a hundred pairs of eyes were watching them?

�™ 🌾 🌾 🌾

Bancroft and Rowan stared at Donald.

"Hello," he said, as though he had just arrived home from a long trip.

"My goodness," said Bancroft. "It's amazing. His fever is gone. Rowan, you're a genius. You found a cure even without the stony lunacrop."

Rowan smiled weakly and hugged Donald. "Welcome back," she whispered. She took his paws and turned them over. They were covered in small pustules.

"Gosh, I'm really hungry," said Donald. "Is there any food around here?"

Donald ate, all the while chitchatting about the dance he'd been learning for the festival and how the last thing he remembered was dancing in the classroom. "I wouldn't be surprised if Dora tripped me up," he said with a grin. "She can't dance for toffee . . . got two left hind legs. Where is she, anyway?"

He looked around him and now noticed the other beds, occupied by his school friends. His snout fell open. "What are they all doing here?" he asked.

Rowan fought back her tears. She explained how sick he had been and how his school friends had also become ill.

"You mean they caught it from me?" His eyes were wide, and his voice trembled.

"It's nobody's fault," Rowan assured him. "It's a sickness. It spreads from one to another; that's how the disease survives."

"Then who did I catch it from? What's wrong with me, anyway?" he asked, looking at his paws.

Rowan couldn't bring herself to speak the name.

"Wolf fever," said Bancroft.

"Oh," Donald said quietly. "You mean the Curse. Our parents were sick with it. The whole tribe had it. I'm going to get sicker, aren't I?" he said in a matter-of-fact voice.

Rowan nodded.

"Will I die like they did?" he asked.

Rowan smothered a sob. "Course you won't die, Donald. Why, Penhaligon is out at this very moment, collecting the herb that we need for the cure. He'll be back very soon." Rowan felt the cub's ears: his fever was cooling. "I want you to tell me, Donald, if you remember being with any other creature who has been sick."

Donald shook his head.

"Did you talk to any strangers? Did you go down the old mine, find something unusual?"

Again Donald shook his head, but more slowly this time.

Bancroft stared at him. "You won't be in any trouble, Donald. We just need to try to find out where the disease came from. After all, no one has seen wolf fever for many a season."

Donald looked out the window. "Where's Dora?"

"She'll be back soon. Now please think, Donald. Bancroft will sit with you while I make up some salve for your paws," said Rowan.

She left Bancroft reading a storybook to Donald and hurried down the spiral steps to the dungeon storeroom. Her footsteps echoed on the hard stone as she crossed to light the lamps hanging on the hewn rock walls. It was cold in the dungeon, and it felt good. The tip of her snout was hot and dry.

She quickly stepped around the wooden cover of

the sea hole to the shelves of healing ingredients. If Penhaligon did not return soon, the poison would spread through Donald's body. There must a way to stop it, something she hadn't thought of. Rowan pulled down box after box of dried herbs and bottles of tinctures and salves, reading labels, remembering little-used cures, racking her brain to come up with something, anything. There must have been something Mennah had taught her that would help. . . .

She was vaguely aware of the dull sound of crashing waves beneath the covered sea hole. Then she heard another sound, like something scraping underneath the wooden cover. She turned quickly, but nothing seemed amiss.

As she sorted through bottles of lotions, the lamps flickered and the temperature in the dungeon suddenly dropped as though she were in an ice cave. Rowan shivered. The noise of the ocean was much louder now, and the air filled with a sudden salty dampness.

Instinctively her hackles rose. Something was behind her. Whatever it was should not be there. No one had followed her into the dungeon. Nothing could climb up from the ocean. The dungeon floor was far too high above the water, and the jagged rocks of the sea cave were too slippery to climb on. But something was there. Rowan knew she must turn around, because whatever it was, it was waiting for *her*.

🕯 🕯 🕯 🕯

"You ain't got a clue where you're going, have you, Penhaligon?" accused Dredge with a sneer.

"Of course I do," said Penhaligon, hoping he did not sound as clueless as he felt. "We're headed toward the three-humped ridge."

"Well, I go no further," said Elgato, "until I have food and a catnap." He sat on a rock. "We cannot see anyway. Eez too dark." He gestured up to the tree-tops.

Alfred and Bert nodded in approval. Even Hotchi looked relieved. Since his legs were shorter than anyone else's, he had to trot twice as fast to keep up with the others.

"We'll take a break until first light," announced Dredge. "Alfred! Bert! Go find fuel for a fire."

"Oh, there's a surprise," grumbled Alfred, and the two crew ferrets went in search of kindling.

The group huddled around a meager fire to eat their bread and dried fish. The fire's glow seemed to make the surrounding forest even darker. Dredge stared into the flames.

Penhaligon watched him closely. He could tell that the ferret captain had something on his mind, and Penhaligon knew that it wouldn't be anything good as far as he was concerned. It wasn't long before Dredge pulled Elgato to one side. The two of them spoke in whispers. As the fox watched, Elgato seemed to question whatever it was Dredge was telling him, but when Dredge raised his voice, Penhaligon heard Elgato reply, "Okay, okay, eez good plan. I like eet."

Penhaligon nudged Hotchi, who was already half-asleep. "We may have to think fast, old friend. Be on your guard. If we have to run for it, head for the beach and hide."

"Right," said Hotchi; then he started to snore.

But no one slept for long.

The howling started just after midnight. Sometimes the sound was so near that the group felt sure they were surrounded. They kept their weapons close-by for fear of attack. Other howls echoed as far away as the mountains. There was no doubt that whatever creatures were making the eerie sound, they inhabited the whole island.

🌱 🌱 🌱 🌱

Gertrude had almost finished cleaning the attic in the apothecary shop. Being there with Penhaligon had reminded her that she'd meant to do the task months ago. It was a dirty job, and even with one of Menhenin's old scarves around her head and her tail tucked into her apron, her chestnut-colored fur was still covered in dust; she'd need a good brushing before she finally fell into bed.

Yawning, she tried to close the lid of Menhenin's old chest, but it jammed. She rearranged the books inside, but still it would not shut properly. The lining of the lid was bulky, as though something was stuck behind it. The fabric had rotted in the corner, and Gertrude gently peeled the frayed edge away from the lid.

"Blithering bats," she breathed when she saw the gilded papers slide from their hiding place. "These look like more pages from the old book."

Gertrude couldn't read the pages but she reasoned that if they had been hidden, they must be important—some secret, perhaps. Any information that could help Penhaligon was crucial. She packed a bag that very night. She'd catch the mail coach from the Warren Arms first thing in the morning.

The Visitor in the Dungeon

A prickle of fear ran down her back, but she, Rowan, had been raised by wolves. She would meet her fate head-on rather than never know what had befallen her. She turned slowly and gasped.

There, poking its silver-scaled neck and massive head through the sea hole, was a sea serpent. The wooden cover was balanced on top of its head, like some eccentric hat. Rowan held on to the mixing table as her hind legs weakened.

"Oh m-m-my," she stammered.

The serpent gazed at her.

"Oh my goodness!" Rowan stood, frozen.

The creature tipped its head, and the cover slid off and crashed to the floor. The serpent snaked toward Rowan and opened its mighty jaws, revealing a forked purple tongue and a set of fine, pointy teeth.

She closed her eyes and silently whispered good-
bye to Penhaligon. But instead of being swept up in
the serpent's jaws, she heard a jingle and a rattle as
something rolled across the floor. She opened her
eyes and picked up the slimy object. It was Princess
Katrina's royal ring.

"Oh my," said Rowan again. She wasn't sure what
to think. Either the serpent had swallowed Penhaligon
and this was all that was left, or it was some kind of
message. She decided to be optimistic. "If you knew
where to find me," she told the serpent, "then perhaps
you know how to find Penhaligon?"

The serpent draped itself across the
stone floor and closed its eyes. Rowan
spotted the wound where Penhaligon had pulled out the
ferret arrow. A dark
liquid oozed from the
puffy-looking gash.

"You poor thing!" she
cried. "This looks like
an arrow wound." She

examined the cut. "Someone has been hunting you, I'd guess." She searched the shelf and took down a container labeled SALVE OF PALM STALK. "Now hold still," she said, thinking to herself that she must be quite mad, attending to a sea serpent that could swallow her in one bite. She emptied the canister, slathering the gooey paste gently over the wound. Several damaged silver scales fell into her paw. "How beautiful you

are," she whispered. "I didn't know serpents still existed. How could anyone hurt you?" She smoothed the creature's neck with salve and began to softly hum the Romany lullaby.

The serpent let out a sigh of air through its nostrils.

"Soothing, isn't it?" said Rowan. "It's an old Romany wolf recipe. Smells nasty, but works like a charm." As she hummed and petted the serpent, Rowan found herself thinking about Penhaligon and how worried he must be not even knowing if Donald was alive or dead. The serpent turned its head and gazed at her. A sudden, clear vision of an island appeared in Rowan's mind, a place covered in dark green forest with a mountainous ridge of three peaks. She did not know this place, but somehow she knew that Penhaligon was there.

"What a very odd feeling," she murmured. "Like someone putting thoughts into my head."

She wrapped the scales in her handkerchief and studied the serpent, staring into its eyes. "Hmm, I think I *have* heard Romany stories told about serpents," she said to herself, recalling Bancroft's question. "But no—not serpents . . . sea dragons. Are you a sea dragon, I wonder? Are there others like you?"

The sea serpent simply gazed at her. The island

vision filled Rowan's head once more, but this time she saw two ships at anchor. "The sea dragons in the stories could talk. You speak . . . without words. Is that how it was?" she asked the serpent. But she received no answers, only the image in her mind. "This must be Howling Island. Can you take a message to Penhaligon?"

Rowan decided there was only one way to find out if the serpent could, in turn, read her thoughts. She scribbled a note.

My dearest Penhaligon,

Please hurry. Donald has the pustules on his paws. The cough will follow soon. Most village young ones have caught a form of the sickness. I do not know how febra lupi has learned to infect them or what course the sickness will take. Villagers are angry and scared. They threaten to leave Porthleven. I don't have to tell you how serious this would be if the fever spreads to other villages. Please hurry home with the stony lunacrop.

Your Rowan

P.S. Dora ran away. I pray she is safe with you.

P.P.S. How I miss you.

Rowan rolled up the note and pressed it into a container. "Please take this to Penhaligon," she said, and concentrated on Penhaligon's face in her mind. Gingerly, she placed the container in the serpent's mouth. The creature rose up and slithered back through the sea hole.

Rowan hummed Mennah's lullaby to herself as she hurriedly made Donald's salve. She couldn't explain it, but as she started up the stone dungeon steps, she felt more hopeful. She would tell Bancroft the wolf tale of the sea dragon. But her encounter with the real serpent would remain her little secret for now, though she would have dearly loved to see the faces of the village elders if they could have set eyes on the creature. She was not sure how she'd explain the smashed sea-hole cover if anyone saw it. But flaming foxgloves! She smiled to herself. She'd think of something.

🕯 🕯 🕯 🕯

The island howlers did not show themselves that night. Finally, as dawn broke, the cries stopped and the ragtag group fell into a fitful sleep. When they woke, Bert and Alfred had disappeared.

"Oh m-m-my," said Hotchi. "Do you think they was taken by the wild things?"

Dredge shrugged. "Who cares? I don't have time to worry about them."

Penhaligon prepared to lead the way, but Dredge suddenly stepped in front of him.

"The plan has changed, Penhaligon. I'm finished looking for your plant. Give me the royal ring."

"We had a deal," said Penhaligon with a growl.

"Not anymore," laughed Dredge. "With the princess's ring, I can tell the Spatavian court any story I wish and pick up any riches due the famous Penhaligon Brush."

Penhaligon looked at Elgato, who shrugged.

Dredge drew his sword. "Give me the ring."

"I don't have it," said Penhaligon.

"Don't lie to me, fox," Dredge warned.

"A gentleman fox never lies," said Penhaligon, and he drew out the chain and locket from his shirt. "See?"

"Search him!" Dredge thundered.

"Eez not here," Elgato almost mewed, after checking the chain around Penhaligon's neck.

"Check his pockets," said Dredge.

The cat patted Penhaligon's pockets up and down, but found only a pocket watch and a grubby handkerchief. "Eez not here."

"You told me he had the ring." Dredge seethed.

"But he did! I saw eet," said Elgato. "He must

have hidden eet on board your sheep. He eez smart fox."

"Is it on the ship?" demanded Dredge.

"Maybe," said Penhaligon with a smirk.

"We can search when we get back," Dredge told Elgato, sword in hand. He took a step toward Penhaligon. "Without you."

Penhaligon thought about drawing his sword and fighting, but he doubted he could defend himself and Hotchi against Elgato and Dredge together. There was only one thing to do.

"Now, Hotchi!" yelled Penhaligon. "Run!" Then the fox sprinted as fast as he could into the forest, heading toward the darkest part of the thicket. He heard Dredge behind him, screaming curses.

Penhaligon's heart thumped and felt ready to burst, but he didn't stop. He followed his instincts and dodged under and over branches, pushing through undergrowth that yanked out clumps of his fur by the roots, until he could no longer hear anyone following. He slowed and eventually stopped, sinking to the ground. He was matted with sweat, and panting so hard, his tongue hung from his mouth. But he'd escaped.

It was only then that he noticed the clearing in front of him. The sun shone through the trees and warmed the earth. There was something odd about the way the plants were growing—not in wild confusion as in other parts of the forest, but in neat rows. On one side of the clearing, there was a pile of root vegetables, ready for storage. They looked like . . . turnips? Penhaligon wandered into the clearing for a better look. They were indeed turnips. A rope ladder was fastened to the trunk of one of the larger trees. High in the tree was a wooden platform shaped like the deck of a ship, with a neat cabin built on top. There were shelters of varying sizes in the other trees also; in fact, in all the trees around him. It was a village of treetop boats.

His tingling spine warned him that he was not alone. Looking into the forest gloom, he saw shadowy figures watching him with fiery red eyes.

Penhaligon swallowed hard. He took a step back but realized, too late, that he was surrounded. The creatures threw back their shaggy heads, one after the other, and sang a chorus of sinister howls.

Hotchi had run only a little way before Elgato caught up with him. "Mister 'Otchi," said Elgato. "There eez a smile on my face to see you run this way on your very leetle legs. I am having the advantage over you, yes?" He pointed his sword to Hotchi's rotund stomach, but then lowered the blade.

"What do you want?" asked Hotchi.

"All I've ever wanted, Mister 'Otchi . . . to be paid my gold, as promised." Elgato began to purr. "I have a plan . . ."

But before he could continue, Dredge appeared from the bushes. "Well done, Elgato—you caught the short, fat one."

Hotchi puffed up his spines with indignation.

"Now then . . . you'd better tell us what Penhaligon did with the ring."

Hotchi looked from Elgato's sword to Dredge's. "Look out behind you!" he yelled.

Dredge and Elgato spun around to see . . . nothing. When they turned back to Hotchi, he had turned himself into a round ball of spines.

"Drat!" Dredge yelled. "If you want to play ball, hedgehog, you've picked the wrong partner. Elgato! Roll him down to the beach."

"But he eez all spiny," complained the cat.

"Then find something to roll him with," growled Dredge.

Elgato found a stick with which to push Hotchi, but still, every so often one of the spines would jab him. "Ouch!" he yelled.

"Hurry up and stop complaining!" snapped Dredge.

When they arrived at the beach, they found that one of the rowboats was missing. "Now, we know where Alfred and Bert got to, those sniveling cowards." Dredge spat. "They'll be sorry when I catch up with them. Roll the hedgehog into the briny, then; if he don't talk, he can join the sea urchins. He looks like one of 'em anyways."

Elgato rubbed his wounds and unhappily pushed Hotchi

into the shallows. "Mister 'Otchi," he whispered. "Eez good idea you unroll yourself. That Dredge, he eez not joking—I have seen him do very bad things."

Hotchi stayed rolled in a tight ball. He could feel the water on his spines. If Elgato kept rolling him, his head would soon be underwater. He wondered how long he could hold his breath.

"Push him in farther," roared Dredge.

"But if he drowns, we'll never find out where eez the ring. It could be anywhere," said Elgato.

"Roll him!" ordered Dredge.

Hotchi was now almost completely submerged.

"The book! Eez good idea! I forgot the beeg book!" shouted Elgato.

"What book?" asked Dredge.

"The fox, he has a book, a very old, precious book. Never let eet out of his sight. Maybe eet eez a clue?" Elgato said hopefully.

"Right, then; push Spiny into the drink and we'll go search aboard the *Jagged Claw*."

"I think we should take Mister Spiny . . . in case eet eez hidden somewhere."

Dredge was thoughtful. "All right. We can always push him overboard later, I s'pose."

Elgato quickly rolled Hotchi back into the

shallows, where the hedgehog unrolled himself, coughing and spluttering.

"What's going on? Are ye trying to drown me?" he rasped.

"I trying to save your life." Elgato hissed and dragged the quivering hedgehog into the remaining rowboat.

"Thank the pigs, you're back!" Pig-wiggy shouted as they climbed aboard the *Jagged Claw.* "Cap'n Dredge, sir! It's the young wolf. She needs the apothecary; she's right poorly." He suddenly realized Penhaligon was not with them. "Where is 'e?"

"Eaten by the wild creatures, hopefully, although he seems to have a knack for avoiding being the main course. Guard this spiny hog, Pig-wiggy." He took Elgato by the shoulder. "Now then. Where's Penhaligon's cabin?"

Hotchi gasped. In all the excitement, he had completely forgotten to hide the gold and the book. Penhaligon had asked him to do one thing, and he'd failed. What more could possibly go wrong?

Elgato led the way belowdecks and shoved open the cabin door. Dredge marched in.

"Go away!" Dora growled weakly from her berth. But Dredge laughed and ignored Dora's snarls. He took hold of Penhaligon's knapsack and shook the contents out on the floor. The linen-wrapped book fell out amongst the jumble of clothes, and with it, Prince Tamar's bag of gold coins.

"I think it's my lucky day!" Dredge felt the weight of gold in the purse, and his lopsided smirk grew broad. He yanked open the book and roughly skimmed through the pages, tearing the delicate old paper.

Elgato cringed as some of the ornate gold-leaf illustrations crumbled to dust. "Eez better to turn page from the top, *Capitán*," he said.

Dredge glared at him. "What?"

The cat swallowed hard and felt a flush of heat. "I mean, eez good to turn the pages from the top, gently. They will not tear and you will not lose any valuable information."

"Oh, right." Dredge leafed slowly through the pages, and from the upper right-hand corner. "Well, well, well," muttered Dredge. "Sea serpents! And like all good books, a map. Do you understand this language, Elgato?"

The cat shook his head.

"Me neither. But I don't need to understand the language to read a map. It's the three-humped ridge of

Howling Island . . . Serpent Ridge. And here's a cave below it. And this . . . It can't be . . ." Dredge suddenly let out a holler. "At last! I'm rich!"

Elgato looked puzzled.

"Ha! You poor fool! You don't realize what this map tells! It shows the prize I've been searching the high seas for. It shows the lair of the sea serpent." Dredge snapped the book shut and patted the dumbfounded cat on the back. "Well done, Elgato. After I have the serpent, your debt is paid; you can have back your crummy ship. My fortune is made. We sail for the three-humped mountain immediately."

P enhaligon stared at the creatures that formed a circle around him. They were taller than he, long-limbed, with shaggy dark fur. Their howls turned his blood ice-cold.

He pulled himself up to full height.

"Stay back!" he commanded, hackles raised. He drew his lips back in a snarl, showing his teeth. He was ready to fight, to the death if necessary. He could not let anyone or anything stop him from his mission.

The creatures moved closer. He could see their ruddy brown eyes now; their fur, gray and black; and their strong snouts with sharp incisor teeth. He drew a sharp breath. He could hardly believe his eyes. "Romany wolves!"

The pack stepped aside to allow one to come forward. He was tall, with sturdy limbs, and he wore a tunic woven of rough but well-made cloth. A braided

silver vine hung around his neck. Penhaligon recognized several silver serpent scales hanging from the pendant.

"What do you want here?" asked the wolf in a deep, menacing voice.

"I don't want trouble." Penhaligon tried not to stammer. Every scary childhood story of the savage Romany wolves streamed through his head. He forced himself to concentrate. He should not fear these creatures: his own father had been a wolf; he had wolf blood in his veins. But he was terrified.

The chief wolf spoke again. "What do you want here?"

"I am an apothecary, on an important mission. I am in search of the herb stony lunacrop to save my son, Donald. He has *febra lupi*, wolf fever."

A murmur traveled around the pack. The large wolf narrowed his eyes and growled. "How can *your* son have wolf fever?"

"He *is* a wolf. He has a sister; she is here with me, on board our ship. They are twin cubs. I adopted them."

"Of what tribe are they?"

"The tribe of the Purple Moor," said Penhaligon.

At this, the wolf approached him and studied

Penhaligon closely. "If what you say is true, that you are seeking help for a Romany wolf cub, then you are welcome." Then he snarled, "But if we find you are here to steal secrets for your own use, you will be very sorry. Come, we will talk."

Penhaligon would rather have continued on his way, but there was nothing else to do but follow the wolf. They climbed one of the ladders attached to a gnarled tree trunk. As the foliage thickened, the light took on a calm pale green hue. Penhaligon smelled the fresh scent of young leaves, and a gentle breeze cooled his ears. He was surprised that such savage creatures chose to live in such peaceful surroundings.

They reached a deck-shaped platform, and Penhaligon could now see that there were more decks even higher up in the branches. Rope ladders hung from these upper branches, where sleeping shelters, covered in cushions of soft grass, were nestled into the limbs. Gangways of planks connected most of the village ship decks, but the one on which he stood was separate. It was also larger and more ornate, with its shelter decorated with carved ships' rails and ocean-worn mastheads. Penhaligon could tell that the pieces had been collected from the beach over the course of many seasons. He looked down. The rest of the pack had silently disappeared back into the forest.

"You will tell me more about how you came to Howling Island. But first, as is our custom of welcome, we shall share food and drink together." The wolf pointed to a large pitcher of water and a bowl. "You may wash here."

Penhaligon realized that he had not looked in a mirror for days. His clothes were filthy, and his fur was encrusted with dried salt crystals. He must look a fearsome sight, and he probably smelled as bad as the ferrets. He

laid down his filthy jacket and unbuttoned his shirt.

"Where did you get that?" demanded the chief
wolf. He stared at Penhaligon as though the fox had
suddenly grown two heads. He pointed at Penhaligon's locket.

"I . . . it was my mother's." Penhaligon placed his
paw protectively over the chain.

The wolf approached Penhaligon
and studied his face with an
amazed expression.

"Tell me your name," he demanded.

Penhaligon had an uncomfortable feeling of riding on a fast wave, being hurtled in an unknown direction. "Penhaligon Brush," he said.

The chief's eyes clouded with distant memories. "Then I am your father, Mawgan," he said.

🪶 🪶 🪶 🪶

Rowan spent the rest of the night wondering whether her encounter with the sea serpent had been real or imagined. She was so very tired; perhaps it had been a dream. But then she felt the thin slivers of scales in her handkerchief and smiled.

The village young ones were still miserable with fever, and itchy pustules were appearing all over their bodies, not just behind the ears. None of them, though, had yet developed the characteristic stare of *febra lupi,* and for that Rowan was grateful. She made careful notes on how the disease was progressing, as she knew Penhaligon would want to learn as much about the sickness as she did. She glanced out the window to the driveway. It was still blazing with pink rhododendrons, and birds were singing in the morning sun. Perhaps today he would return.

Bancroft arrived with breakfast, and as they sipped

their nettle tea, the badger listened to Rowan's recollection of the sea-dragon stories from her childhood.

"From what I can remember, the wolves held the sea dragon in the greatest regard. They cared for it. The sea dragons were their protectors. They would keep the wolves from harm by telling them when enemies were approaching."

"Telling?"

"They spoke . . . in the stories."

"Ha! Well, it goes some way to proving our theory that at one time the Romany wolves had a strong connection with sea serpents. It's quite fascinating. I'm not sure I'd go so far as to believe that sea dragons could actually talk! Isn't it wonderful how these stories are passed down from generation to generation, each adding its own embellishment in order to tell a good tale!" He chuckled.

At that moment there was a knock at the door. Bancroft went to answer it, still shaking his head. "Talking dragons! That's a good one." He was surprised to see Gertrude standing on the doorstep on that sunny morning, overnight bag at her feet.

"Why, bless me," he said. "I am happy to see you, Gertrude, but I have to warn you, the hospital is under quarantine."

"Yes, they told me in the village. Folk are saying that the Curse of the Romany Wolves has come back to haunt them. They also say that Penhaligon has deserted them. I don't believe it!"

"Nor should you. It's a very difficult time, Gertrude. It is true that *febra lupi* has sickened the young ones. We don't know what the outcome will be. But Penhaligon has not deserted us; he has traveled to Spatavia to find the herb needed for the cure."

"Oh dear," said Gertrude. "Rowan didn't have the stony lunacrop?"

"She'd never even heard of it." Bancroft shook his head sadly. "We had hoped that by now we would have had a message from Penhaligon or the Spatavian court."

"Well, this might be something." She handed Bancroft an envelope. "I hitched a ride with the mail coach early this morning. The driver said this was for Ferball Manor, so I offered to give it to you."

She bent down to her bag and pulled out the pages she'd found.

"And I found these hidden in Menhenin's old trunk, which is really why I'm here. They look like more pages from that old book. I thought they might be important."

Bancroft looked them over with interest. "I wonder why they were hidden? I'd better study all this in the library," he said, shaking his large head. "Thank you for coming, Gertrude. You'd best leave now."

"You can't get rid of me that easily, Bancroft! I don't care if the hospital is quarantined; I'm here to help," said Gertrude, picking up her bag and stepping into the foyer. "But tell me, why are the villagers so angry? Rowan is an excellent apothecary. They must know she is doing everything possible to help."

Bancroft sighed. "They think Donald is to blame for the spread of the disease. But it's not his fault that *febra lupi* has learned how to infect other creatures. We were to hold a meeting in the schoolhouse to try to explain, but I have been too busy. Most of the youngsters are now sick with the fever. There have been new cases every hour. Rowan is exhausted, and there doesn't seem to be a cure that works."

The badger sighed again. "I thought Donald seemed better, but Rowan assures me that it's temporary and that he will become very ill, very soon, and perhaps may even . . ." Bancroft's words trailed off.

Gertrude didn't need to hear the rest. She knew the way the fever broke just before the poison spread through the body.

"You must go, Gertrude. We mustn't take the risk that another apothecary might get sick," said Bancroft.

"Rowan is sick?" Gertrude looked worried.

"She won't admit it," said Bancroft, "but she looks thoroughly exhausted, and she won't take a break from the ward at all. She's even been sleeping in there."

"Then I'm definitely not going anywhere, Bancroft. It sounds like you need all the help you can get."

The badger smiled and took Gertrude's bag. "Thank you, Gertrude. Rowan is on the ward. I must read this letter. It bears Prince Tamar's royal seal."

The young fox was shocked when she walked into the ward. Every hospital bed was occupied. There were even some creatures sleeping on the floor, on makeshift mattresses. There was a strong smell of bog mud, and the ward was heavy with silent sickness— except for a sob coming from one of the beds.

Gertrude went to investigate. A rabbit lay in the bed, her soft coat dark from the sweat of fever. "There, there, now," said Gertrude. "Can I get you a drink of water?"

The small, forlorn rabbit looked up at her with dull, dry eyes. "I want my mommy," she whispered. "Where's my mommy? Please find her."

Rowan quietly touched Gertrude on the shoulder

and smiled her welcome. "There now," Rowan told the young rabbit. "Mommy will be here very soon, you'll see."

"Oh, Rowan, I had no idea things were this bad. Why didn't you send for me?"

"It all happened so quickly." Rowan hugged Gertrude. "But I'm so glad you're here."

Gertrude peeked at Donald, who was sleeping soundly. "You have been through so much, and look at your poor paws," said Gertrude as she saw the raw, red-stained flesh. "I shall wash up and put on my apron, and then you, my dear Rowan, will sit down and have a rest whilst I do the next round of bog-mud poultice."

Rowan smiled weakly. "Thank you, Gertrude. I expect you could do with a rest yourself after your trip."

Gertrude had finished singing the little rabbit off to sleep and she and Rowan were catching up when Bancroft came hurrying into the ward, his brow furrowed.

"Rowan, Gertrude—it's a letter from Prince Tamar. Penhaligon never arrived in Spatavia. He was never on the ship. It sailed without him."

Rowan's head began to spin in dizzy confusion. "But then where is he?" Her eyes widened. "And where's Dora?"

Just then, there was a pounding on the manor door, which burst open, spilling a crowd of villagers into the hallway. They jostled and pushed each other, full of self-importance, each wanting to get in the front. Rowan saw Bill Goat trying to stay unnoticed behind everyone else. This time, it was the stoat who spoke. He pointed at Bancroft.

"You 'ave not called your schoolhouse meeting, Brock, so we called one of our own. We're taking our young 'uns and leaving Porthleven, where there ain't any infectious Romany wolves."

There was a murmur of agreement from the crowd.

Rowan gasped. "But you can't—they are sick. Traveling will just make them worse."

"They won't be no sicker than they are here, Mistress Rowan. And they'll be away from that . . . wolf. We'll find someone who *knows* what they're doing and can cure them."

"But you'll give the disease a chance to find new victims!" cried Rowan. "It'll be worse. You can't be so selfish!"

"Are we supposed to sit 'ere and wait for it to get us too?" someone in the crowd shouted. Fists were raised. "You can't cure them. We need to find someone who can."

At that moment, Gertrude walked out from the ward. The crowd took a step back. Donald was walking by her side. Rowan knew that he could hardly stand on his own. The effort he was making must be incredible.

"Hello, everybody," he said in a small voice.

The crowd hushed.

"I'm sorry you have lost faith in Mistress Rowan,

your apothecary," said Gertrude. "Not one of you stopped to ask how Donald was doing, so I thought maybe you'd like to see for yourselves. As you can see, he's much better, and it's all due to Rowan's skill and excellent care."

"But, Gertrude . . . ," Rowan began. She was quieted by Gertrude's look. She caught on to Gertrude's game. "Oh . . . that's right. Donald is feeling much better. It'll just be a matter of time before all the young ones work through their fevers. They are perfectly safe here and well cared for, but if any of you wish to take your sons or daughters away, then please go ahead. They shouldn't get too much sicker if you wrap them up warmly." Rowan stepped aside. "Hopefully they won't infect you and the rest of your families."

No one in the crowd moved.

"Well then," said Bancroft. "I suggest you all go back to the village and let us take care of your offspring."

As Bancroft shut the door on the last villager, Donald sagged against Gertrude's legs. Rowan rushed over, dropped to her knees, and hugged him.

"Donald, that was such a brave thing to do. I know how hard it was for you to walk after having been in bed for so long."

The young cub managed a weak grin. "It was

Gertrude's idea. She said you needed some help. Can I go back to bed now, please?"

Bancroft carried Donald back to his bed. The badger looked stern. "I don't like fooling the villagers like that, but I agree it was necessary. We may have avoided a catastrophe—thanks to you, young Donald," he said. Then he added, "But it won't be long before the villagers realize what's really happening. We need help. We're not even sure if Penhaligon will return with the stony lunacrop anytime soon. I shall contact Prince Tamar immediately; he needs to know the situation."

Help came much sooner than they expected, and not exactly in the way they had planned. The Royal Warthog Guard arrived to quarantine the whole village. No creature was allowed to leave or was let in to visit. Even Rowan and Bancroft had been warned not to leave the manor under any circumstances. All villagers had to be behind closed doors by the dusk curfew, and all plans for the future Ferball Festival were canceled. For the second time in its history, the village of Porthleven was under siege.

The Serpent's Lair

"Well, that's it!" shouted Pig-wiggy. "I've just about 'ad it with the likes of 'im." He jumped up and down, shaking his fist, as he watched Dredge, Elgato, and Hotchi row over to Dredge's ship, leaving him on board with the sick wolf cub. "I've 'ad enough of you ferrets. You all stink, anyway!" he shouted.

But nobody heard him. Dredge

was too busy thinking about what kind of trap he would lay for the sea serpent. He was singing to himself.

"Capitan Dredge," said Elgato. "You have many high spirits?"

Dredge gave a lopsided scowl. "Elgato, I may even be in a good enough mood to give you one of the silver scales from the serpent. Just a small one, mind."

"Most generous," hissed the cat under his breath, but he purred despite himself. "And how do you intend to keel thees serpent with eets armor of silver? Eez true eet can swallow two creatures at a time—three, if eet crunches them up first?"

Hotchi winced. He had kept silent ever since he had unrolled from a spiny ball. He was furious with himself for not having hidden the book as Penhaligon had asked. Now his friend was lost on Howling Island, probably captured—or something worse—by wild creatures, and Hotchi had no doubt that Dredge would throw him over the side whenever the thought struck him. And what would happen to Dora? He was no apothecary, but even he could guess why Dora was sick. Donald would die without the cure. He had to face it. He had failed miserably in their mission. He might as well save Dredge the job and throw himself overboard—he deserved it.

The *Black Shriek* sailed out through the reef, and the ferrets cheered and sang as word of newfound wealth spread across the decks.

Hotchi said yet another silent good-bye to his friend Penhaligon.

❦ ❦ ❦ ❦

Penhaligon felt as though the blood had suddenly drained from his head, leaving a swirling confusion. He sat and tried to make sense of what the wolf had just told him. "My parents are dead," he said finally.

"This is a shock for me too," said Mawgan. "I had always hoped for a day when I would be reunited with my son. But I never once dared to dream that it would come true. I will tell you my story, Penhaligon, and I would like to hear yours. Finish your washing." He pointed to the pitchers of water. "When you are comfortable, we shall talk."

As Penhaligon washed the salt from his fur, he put the wolf's words aside and thought about his nice deep bathtub back at Ferball Manor instead. Rowan and Bancroft would never imagine where his travels had taken him. He was willing to listen to this wolf—he would need his help to find the stony lunacrop—but the chief must be mistaken. There was no way this stranger could be his father. If he were, Penhaligon would know it; he would feel it, somehow. But what a fireside tale he'd have to tell Rowan and Bancroft . . . if he ever saw them again.

Mawgan was sitting beside a feast of roast turnips, fruit, and fresh grilled fish. Penhaligon's mouth watered at the aroma, and he realized he couldn't remember the last time he'd eaten a proper meal.

"Sit," said Mawgan. "Eat, and I shall begin. First I will tell you about your mother. She was the kindest, most gentle creature I ever met. Her fur was so soft—the color of ripe chestnuts, I always thought."

Penhaligon felt the locket. It still held a bit of his mother's and father's fur. The fox fur was indeed the ruddy chestnut color the wolf had described. Penhaligon's heart beat a little faster.

Mawgan's eyes grew distant. "I'm sure Violet Brock told you much about why we had to leave."

"No," Penhaligon growled. "Everything was kept secret from me until just a few seasons ago, after Mrs. Brock passed away. I did not even know that the creature who took me into his apothecary practice was actually my own grandfather."

"Menhenin, a Romany wolf, was accepted by village creatures?" Mawgan was clearly astonished.

Penhaligon grimaced. "It's a long story."

Mawgan's look suddenly turned to one of horror. "But, Penhaligon, if you were told nothing, you must have thought we abandoned you!"

Penhaligon sighed. "Go on with your story," he said.

"Yes, you deserve that, at the very least," Mawgan said sadly. "We loved each other very much, your mother and I," he said quietly. "But other creatures would not accept us. Even my own father sent us away. He was already disappointed that I had no interest in following in his footsteps as tribal healer. When I told him I wanted to take a fox as my bride, he was horrified. He told me he would never allow it. So we ran away, far away up north, where the lord of a manor married us under a chill lakeside moon. And we were happy."

The wolf's wistful smile left his face. "But it was a very lonely and hard life for your mother, who had always been surrounded by friends and had always known the comforts of hearth and hot bath."

Penhaligon smiled—he too loved his own home comforts.

Mawgan continued. "So we decided to search for a land we'd heard about. A new land where creatures accepted you for who you were, not who they thought you ought to be. But then we had joyous news—you were soon to be born. There was no one to help in that lonely place, so we traveled back to the Purple Moor to visit my aunt. She was the birthing wolf of the Romany wolf tribe."

The knot in Penhaligon's stomach tightened. "What was your aunt's name?"

"Mennah was her name. She was always so kind to us, unlike my own father. I still miss her."

As Mawgan's tale unfolded, more puzzle pieces dropped into place, and Penhaligon realized that his family had been closer than he had ever imagined.

"After you were born," continued Mawgan, "things got worse. We were still outcasts. Your mother's health was fragile. We did not want our child to grow up always shunned, made to feel different, so we decided to search for the new land. Your mother wanted to take you with us, but you were so young and she was so frail, I convinced her to leave you behind. We would return for you when you were older, and strong enough to make the journey. I have had to live with the consequences of that decision all my life."

Mawgan stared into his cup of water before gulping it down. "When Menhenin refused to take you, Violet Brock, who was your mother's best friend, took you in and promised to care for you as her own."

Penhaligon was silent for a while. He walked to the window and stared through the peaceful green canopy of his father's home, for now there could be no doubt that this wolf, Mawgan, was indeed his father.

Rowan woke with a start, not quite sure where she was. She sighed, remembering that she had sat down to rest by the great hearth in the Ferball Manor library. She sipped her cup of now cold nettle tea. The sharp taste burned her raw sore throat, but after a while she felt comforted. Bancroft was working at the desk by the window, translating more of the pages Gertrude had brought.

"Oh, Bancroft, you shouldn't have let me doze off. I should check on the patients," Rowan said.

Bancroft looked up from his work. "You shall do no such thing, Rowan. You have not stopped nursing the young ones, and I know you are unwell. You hide it, but I know you." Bancroft could not hide his concern. "I'm glad that you slept, for I have a clue about the cure—now I'm certain." Rowan stepped over to his desk to look at the ancient pages.

"It seems," continued Bancroft, "that the history of the sea serpent—or sea dragons, if you like—and the Romany wolves goes back some time." He pointed to the delicate illustrations of serpents on the pages. "I'm sure there is much to learn from the book that Penhaligon took with him, but here it says that

an ingredient used in many recipes was 'the powdered shell of the serpent,' if I have my translation
right."

Rowan thought for a minute. In all her experience
and learning from Mennah, powdered eggshell had
never been added to anything other than cures for the
stomach. "Well, it was not mentioned in the cure for
febra lupi, but I will try anything. The closest ingredient I have to serpent shell is powdered snake shell. I
shall mix a cure right now, but without the stony
lunacrop, I don't have much hope."

She hesitated as she stepped into the hallway.
"Bancroft, do you think Penhaligon and Dora are all
right?"

"We must prepare for the unexpected and hope for
the best. None of us thought things would turn out
the way they have. For example, I did not expect
Prince Tamar to put Porthleven under guard." Bancroft looked thoughtful. "The warthogs are taking
their duty very seriously. They are arresting anyone
who breaks the rules. The Stoat family was caught
trying to sneak out of the village and is being held in
the schoolhouse. When I complained to the captain of
the guard, he told me his orders were clear. Until a
cure is found, we are all prisoners—even us."

Rowan felt a sudden dryness in her throat. She must find a cure. They could not rely on Penhaligon's return. As she headed for the dungeon, she could not help the tears that stung her soft brown eyes.

§ § § §

Hotchi rolled his eyes as the ferret crew burst into another chorus of a tuneless sea shanty, singing in time to the rowing beat. The sail to Serpent Ridge had been one big celebration. Every ferret on board had a plan of how he was going to spend his share of the fortune. The bow ferrets sharpened their arrows and checked their swords. Dredge was in such a jovial mood that even Bert and Alfred had been spared punishment for deserting their post on Howling Island.

The wind was in their favor, and the *Black Shriek* circled the island in good time. The three-humped ridge loomed above them as they anchored the ship. Dredge studied the sheer rock with his spyglass. It looked solid, with no obvious sign of a cave, but on closer inspection he noticed that at the base of the rock face, a small shelf of stone jutted up from the water. It blended into the main cliff so well, it was practically invisible. He opened the book and checked the map.

"I have to thank you, little fat spiny creature," said Dredge. "If we didn't have the map, I would never in a million seasons have known there was a cave hidden in the cliffs. Now, all thanks to you, the serpent will be slain and we shall be rich." His eyes narrowed as he added, under his breath, "Well, some of us will."

Hotchi was desperate. He didn't know much about sea serpents, but he felt in his spines that there was a reason why the one in the Gassaro Sea had not eaten Penhaligon. He also guessed that the serpent's lair would not have been included in the Romany wolf book if it had not been important. Dredge must be stopped, but how could Hotchi, a hedgehog with such little legs, fight against a whole shipload of ferrets?

"Launch the boats!" screamed Dredge. Within minutes, two rowboats splashed into the water. After one boat was loaded with bow ferrets, Dredge ordered Hotchi and Elgato into the other boat with him. "You will come too," he said, smiling at their surprised faces. "You wouldn't want to miss the fun."

They had rowed a little way from the ship when Elgato tried to reason with Dredge. "Are you sure thees eez a good idea? How you know when eez the serpent coming at his house? Eet could be days and days, no?"

"We'll wait until he does," growled Dredge.

Halfway to the cliff face, Elgato tried again. "Surely eez better for your brave bow ferrets to be doing their shooting without us in the way?"

"Don't worry, you won't be in the way." Dredge smiled.

Hotchi began to sense Elgato's discomfort. He too had an uneasy, queasy feeling. He couldn't fight a sea serpent. He had no skills as a bowman. Why would Dredge have wanted him to come along?

They were nearly at the cliff, and Elgato tried one last time. "Maybe the serpent eez already there. The bow ferrets should go first," he said.

"Getting cold paws?" asked Dredge. "You are both very necessary to my plan," he hissed. "In fact, you play the most important part."

The secret entrance was hidden behind the jutting rock, just as the map had shown. They rowed into the mouth of the dark cave. Even the bow ferrets were silent. They readied their arrows, prepared for anything. Hotchi's spines were pale. He had already seen the size of the sea serpent's jaws and had no doubt that killing it was not going to be as easy as Dredge seemed to think. He noticed Elgato clinging to the side of the boat and realized that the cat was just as scared as he.

As they rowed through the cave, the smell of salty,

rotted weed and dead fish was almost overpowering. There was a ledge of rock at the rear, littered with bones: heaps of nibbled skeletons from season upon season of serpent snacks. Hotchi recognized that many of the bones were the remains of large fish, but some did not look like fish skeletons. He shuddered to think to whom the bones had belonged when they had been covered with flesh. At the widest part of the ledge was a jumbled tower of driftwood logs and dried seaweed.

"Must be the nest," whispered Dredge. "And it looks like no one's home. We'll just have to . . . Wait a minute!" Dredge gasped. "Where's that glow coming from?" He drew the boat as close as he could to the wooded pile. Dredge peered through the jumbled branches. Suddenly he let out a whoop that echoed around the cave. "Even better than I'd hoped!"

Hotchi peered between the layers of logs. His jaw dropped open in surprise. Sitting inside the nest, partially covered by seaweed, was the largest golden egg he had ever seen. Elgato had seen it too. He purred so loudly that Hotchi had to shout to make himself heard: "I think we should leave while we still can!"

Mawgan's Tale

Penhaligon felt that he'd finally found a great treasure, but now wasn't sure if he wanted it anymore. The young cub still somewhere deep inside him needed to howl, to tell his father how unhappy he'd been: how the teasing at school had left him crying alone at night; how knowing that his own parents had left him had caused a wound that would never heal. But he was not a cub anymore, so he simply looked at his father and said, "I waited for you to come back for me for years. Then I no longer waited."

Mawgan looked pained. "We cannot change the past, Penhaligon, however much we'd like to. We can only hope to learn from it. Will you hear the rest of my story?"

Penhaligon nodded and listened to Mawgan's tale: a great storm had torn his parents' ship apart and

Mawgan and his mother had been left floating on a makeshift raft in the Gassaro Sea.

"I don't know how long we were in the water," said Mawgan. "Your mother was so brave. All she thought about was how lucky it was that you were safe with Violet Brock and that you would have a life of calm and quiet in Ramble-on-the-Water."

Penhaligon laughed to himself. His life had been so calm and quiet in Ramble-on-the-Water that at times he thought he'd die of boredom. "But how did you come to be here, on Howling Island?" he asked.

"We were so hot, and a terrible thirst almost sent us mad," continued Mawgan. "The weed wrapped around our legs, trying to pull us under the water's surface. And I must admit, the cool depths seemed like a peaceful end to the blistering heat. But your mother wouldn't let me give up."

Penhaligon thought with a shiver of his own experience in the Gassaro Sea. He knew exactly how his parents must have felt.

"Then," said Mawgan, "the water began to churn and bubble and the silver neck of a sea serpent rose from it. We thought for sure this was the end. But the strangest thing happened. I'll never know why I did, but I started to hum a tune, a lullaby that your grandfather Menhenin used to sing to me. The serpent heard it and was calm, as though it had come to help us, not harm us."

Penhaligon guessed that the tune would have been the same lullaby he had found himself singing when he had first met the serpent. What a very odd coincidence. He suddenly thought of Bancroft, who always said, "There's no such thing as coincidence, Penhaligon; there is always a reason."

"We sat atop our raft," said Mawgan, "not knowing if we were even headed for land, but after what seemed like hours we sighted Howling Island. The serpent pushed us to the shallows, and the Romany wolves that lived here found us, exhausted and close to death. They cared for us and offered us a place among them. We had finally found the place we'd been looking for." Penhaligon's father hung his head. "But at great cost." Mawgan stood up and gazed out the window, deep in thoughts too painful to share. Penhaligon knew he had to ask.

"Where is my mother?"

"We tried for years to find a way home to fetch you. But ships steer a wide berth from Howling Island. No one ever came, so we could not reach you or even send word. Eventually we had to accept that we would never see you again. Your mother became more and more frail. Finally she died of a broken heart."

Penhaligon almost knew that the words were coming, but that did not stop the sting of disappointment nor the tears that filled his eyes.

"I'm sorry, Penhaligon."

The fox drew a deep breath and roughly wiped his tears away. "I do not understand the events that have led to our meeting. But the stage is set for another tragedy unless I can find the cure for a very ill wolf cub. I need the herb stony lunacrop and a way to return home. Will you help me?"

Mawgan nodded. "There is much you should know about the cure for wolf fever. But first tell me, how did you find your way to Howling Island and who are the creatures that arrived with you?"

Penhaligon told Mawgan of Donald's illness, of finding Menhenin's book and realizing they needed stony lunacrop. He explained how he and Hotchi had missed the Spatavian ship, thus ending up with Elgato; he told of stowaway Dora, his encounter with the serpent, and his fateful meeting with the ferret captain, Dredge.

"You have had much adventure already, Penhaligon.

But this book—is it safe at Ferball Manor?" Mawgan asked quietly.

"Actually, I brought it with me. There were maps and illustrations I thought I might need to refer to." He knew when he saw Mawgan's face that this had been the wrong decision.

"Where is the book now?"

"On the *Jagged Claw*. Don't worry, it's safely hidden," Penhaligon assured Mawgan, but he had an uneasy feeling all the same.

"Penhaligon, I need to see it. If it is what I think it is, the book of Romany wolf legend, it must not be found. Those maps show the lairs of sea serpents . . . there are many who seek their silver scales. We believe the Howling Island serpent may be the last of its kind. If it is killed, it will mean the end of the sea serpents forever and, in turn, the end of the Romany wolves."

Penhaligon felt the blood drain from the scruff of his neck. "Flaming foxgloves!"

🕯 🕯 🕯 🕯

Rowan stared at the empty jar of powdered snake shell. How could it be possible? She scowled as she remembered she'd given the last of it to Bill Goat for his stomachaches. She pulled her shawl around her against the clammy sea air. The shattered remains of the sea-hole cover still lay on the floor, and she heard the waves pounding against the rocks far below. The weather had turned stormy once again, and the winds whipped the water into a frenzy.

There would be snake shells over by Rock Pool Lighthouse, she was sure. Normally she would have asked Donald to collect some, as he knew the best snake holes, the ones dotting the faces of the cliffs. Donald was fearless and agile. He could balance on the narrowest ledge while twisting his arm into a hole, all the while laughing.

She smiled sadly. "This time, I shall have to go myself," she said.

Bancroft was dozing by the fire in the library. Rowan smiled as she heard his loud snores. Poor Bancroft; he was exhausted too.

She opened the front door and requested to speak with the captain of the guard.

" 'Fraid not. Orders is orders," he said when she explained that she needed to make a trip to the Rock Pool cliffs.

"But I need those shells to make the cure." She tried to keep her voice even but could feel the anger rising in her chest.

"The best I can do is send a messenger to the prince. If he says it's all right, then you can go," said the captain.

"But that could take hours!" Rowan snapped. "We don't have hours."

"Those are my orders, ma'am," he said curtly.

Rowan slammed the door in frustration. She was not about to accept no for an answer. She needed to get to the Rock Pool cliffs. It would not be easy, with the warthogs patrolling outside Ferball Manor and around the village. This would have to be done in secret.

She grabbed her half-sword from the little cupboard in the foyer and ran upstairs to her bedroom. It had been Lady Ferball's room, and Rowan had kept it just the way Lady Ferball had left it, with its powder-blue drapes and bedcovers. The carved stone fireplace was cold; there had been no time for the luxury of a fire, with so many patients to nurse. Through the bay window that overlooked the garden, Rowan could see only one guard, but she knew there would be more on the roof.

Quickly, she flung open the bottom drawer of her chest and pulled out a knitted sweater, followed by a brown paper package tied with a pink bow.

When she had gathered everything, she placed it all on the bed.

The secret passage that led from Lady Ferball's bedroom to the garden greenhouse had not been used since Sir Derek had occupied the house. Rowan used all her weight to push open the wood panel that concealed the passage. There was a loud groan as it finally gave in to her shoving. Cobwebs hung down in great dusty clumps, and Rowan screwed up her muzzle. There were sure to be more cobwebs, plus who knew what else, in the ancient tunnel.

She checked the garden again. Rain was rolling down the windowpanes, but the guard had gone . . . this was going to be easier than she had thought. She read the card on the paper package, as she had done many times before:

FOR OUR NEXT ADVENTURE . . .
YOURS AND FOREVER,
PENHALIGON

She opened the package and held up a pair of britches. This

particular part of the adventure she would have to undertake without him.

🕯 🕯 🕯 🕯

Two wolf scouts, panting and excited, shouted up to the ship house to tell Mawgan that only the *Jagged Claw* remained anchored in the bay. The other ship was sailing toward Serpent Ridge.

"Send reinforcements to the ridge," Mawgan commanded.

"They are already on their way," said one of the scouts. "But I fear the ship will arrive long before they do."

"That must not happen," said Mawgan. "The lair must be protected at all costs."

The scouts ran swiftly into the woods, leaving Mawgan pacing the floor. "This is worse than I had expected," he said.

Penhaligon thought for a moment. "You are only guessing that Dredge has found the book. It may just be a coincidence that the *Black Shriek* is sailing in that direction. Shouldn't we check aboard the *Jagged Claw* first?"

"I don't believe in coincidence," Mawgan growled.

"You should meet Bancroft, my brother," murmured Penhaligon.

"But you are right, we should check to see if the book is safe."

"But, Mawgan, you cannot go. Remember Dora. Hotchi said that she was not feeling well. I have not been able to examine her. . . . You should not take any chances."

"You think she has the fever?" asked Mawgan.

Penhaligon nodded.

"Then we shall take this with us." Mawgan unlocked a cupboard in the corner of his shelter. He took a small silver flask from the shelf inside. "Here." He gave it to Penhaligon. "This is a bottle of cure for *febra lupi* . . . the *last* bottle."

"What? How can this be the last bottle?"

Mawgan sighed. "We too have to gather the ingredients to make the cure and they are rare."

Penhaligon held the flask like it was the most precious gift. "You are giving it to me? What if anyone here should need it?"

"If the book is safe and our secrets kept, we Romany wolves will be able to mix more of the cure. But be warned, Penhaligon, this bottle contains only enough cure for one creature."

"But both the cubs are sick . . . ," Penhaligon started.

Mawgan put his paw on the fox's shoulder. "There is only enough for one."

Without a word, Penhaligon slipped the precious medicine into his pocket and followed Mawgan down the ladder and through the forest. The path they took was so much easier than the tangled undergrowth they'd had to hack through. As the sunlight filtered more strongly through the thinning canopy of trees, Penhaligon could tell they were nearing the beach. Sure enough, the white sand was soon before them and the sun sparkled on the blue water in an almost blinding flash.

The *Jagged Claw* was still anchored off the coast. Penhaligon's heart sank when he saw that neither rowboat had been left on the beach. "We'll have to swim out to the ship," he said.

"Maybe not," said Mawgan. He pointed to a place where the water boiled and churned. Clouds of sand rolled to the surface.

"What is it?" gasped Penhaligon.

"Our ride to the ship," said Mawgan, and he ran into the shallows.

The serpent raised its head and let out a roar.

"Mawgan! Watch out!" yelled Penhaligon. But it was too late. The serpent coiled around Mawgan and dragged the wolf underwater. Penhaligon ran to help, his sword drawn. Just then Mawgan rose from the water as if by magic. Higher and higher he went. Penhaligon's snout dropped open. Then Mawgan laughed. The fox realized that his father was standing, balanced, on top of the serpent's head.

"Flaming foxgloves, Mawgan . . . I thought . . ."

"Ha!" Mawgan, still laughing, climbed off the serpent's head and settled on its neck. "Sorry, Penhaligon. I couldn't resist showing you our little trick. She loves to show off."

"She?" Penhaligon managed a weak smile.

"Yes, she." Mawgan bared his claws and scratched the serpent behind her ears. The serpent let out a soft sound of pleasure.

"We are the Keepers of this serpent, Penhaligon. Our responsibility as Romany wolves is to care for her. She needs a special herb to keep her silver scales healthy. We grow it for her."

"Stony lunacrop?" Penhaligon asked.

"I'm happy that my son is so smart." Mawgan smiled. "The elders of the Howling Island tribe arrived many seasons past, when she was a hatchling from the old country—your country. They brought the herb with them to cultivate here on the island, as it did not seem to be thriving in the homeland. Some of the elders worried that if the herb stopped growing altogether, there could be a catastrophe. It was a part of Romany wolf history that I knew nothing about, until I was told it by the elders of the island."

"So I've come all the way here and stony lunacrop grows at home?"

"I cannot answer that. You would have to ask a Romany wolf from your country."

Penhaligon realized that his father didn't know that the Purple Moor tribe had died out. He would have to tell him. But not now.

"The elders spoke of a book that had been left behind," said Mawgan. "The book that maybe you have now brought to us. So you see? Secrets were kept from me also. Menhenin must have reasoned that as I refused to become a tribal healer and was determined to leave the moor, the knowledge should

not be passed on to me. How ironic that I ended up here, eh?

"Anyway, the serpent has lived here safely with the tribe . . . until now. Come, she won't harm you; she knows you're one of us."

Penhaligon gingerly stepped onto the serpent's back and found a firm seat between two dorsal fins running down her spine. He held tight as they skimmed across the water at lightning speed. He had never traveled so fast in his life. In just a few seconds, they had reached the *Jagged Claw*.

Mawgan laughed out loud. "How did you like the ride?"

Penhaligon was speech-
less, but he nodded,
grinning.

The serpent
snaked the top
half of her

body over the side of the ship to allow Mawgan and Penhaligon to jump onto the deck.

Pig-wiggy hurried up from below to see what all the noise was about. Mind-boggled, he looked first at the serpent and then at the tall, shaggy wolf. With his stiff Mohawk straight in the air from fright, he ran, squealing, to jump overboard. Mawgan and Penhaligon couldn't help but laugh.

"Pig-wiggy!" Penhaligon called after him. "Stop! It's all right. Don't jump!"

Pig-wiggy looked over his shoulder. "They said you was done for, Penhaligon. That the wild things gotcha."

"Just a nasty rumor, Pig-wiggy! Allow me to introduce my father, the chief 'wild thing.'"

Pig-wiggy swallowed hard and made a little half bow, half curtsey. "Well, I s'pose that's all right, then." But he kept one eye on the serpent and noticed when she dropped something onto the deck. It rolled into a shadowy corner, lost from sight. The serpent, to his relief, then sank back over the side and headed off in the direction of Serpent Ridge.

"I'm glad you've come, Penhaligon. They've all gone and left me and the young wolf—she's right poorly."

"Where is she?"

"In your cabin. I tried me best to make her comfy, but she won't eat, and her eyes are funny-looking."

Penhaligon felt a stab of alarm. "And Hotchi?"

"They took 'im. Cap'n Dredge was in a right tearing 'urry."

"Mawgan, you should stay here. If she does have the fever, you must not catch it." Penhaligon hurried below.

In the dim cabin, he heard Dora's snuffles. He stepped over the mess of his clothes, still in a heap where Dredge had emptied them onto the floor.

"Penhaligon!" she cried when she saw him. "I want to go home, Penhaligon. I want Rowan. I want to see Donald."

Penhaligon examined Dora. Sure enough, she was running a fever, and behind her ears were the telltale swellings. Soon the stare would come to her and she would sink into an unconscious sleep. "Don't worry, Dora. We'll be home soon." He touched the silver bottle of cure in his pocket. She wasn't too sick yet. Perhaps they would be able to mix more cure in time. He must wait awhile. He need not choose yet. "Try to sleep, Dora. I have help with me—a wolf, like you. We are going to find the stony lunacrop right now to take back to Donald. We'll make him well again."

Dora sighed and closed her eyes, a little smile on her face.

"Dora," he whispered. "Before you sleep, can you tell me where Hotchi hid the book and the gold?"

"Dredge took it all," she muttered sleepily.

CHAPTER FIFTEEN

Master Pig-wiggy

Back on deck, Penhaligon found Mawgan pacing impatiently.

"Did you find it?" the wolf demanded.

Penhaligon shook his head. "Dora says that Dredge took it with him. She's very sick, Mawgan. Are you *sure* there isn't any more of the cure on the island? Some that maybe someone has forgotten about?"

"I am sure. As I told you, we have been waiting to make new batches. We must go to the serpent's lair immediately."

"Why can't you prepare some now? You have the stony lunacrop, don't you?" Penhaligon insisted.

Mawgan shook his head. "You must trust me, Penhaligon. I don't have time to explain everything. All I can tell you is that we have everything that's needed for the cure except for the key ingredient. If this Dredge creature finds the lair, we may never have it."

He pointed to the three-humped ridge in the distance. "It will take several hours to get there on foot. We must leave now."

Penhaligon had no other choice but to trust him. He looked around the *Jagged Claw* and then at Pig-wiggy. "Mawgan, it'll be much faster by sea. Master Pig-wiggy, can you sail this ship with just the three of us?"

Pig-wiggy squealed in delight. "Do gulls like herring? Mr. Penhaligon, Mr. Mawgan! Raise the anchor!"

The gentle breeze pushed the *Jagged Claw* across the reef while Pig-wiggy, standing on a barrel, steered the ship. His eyes were bright with excitement as he navigated the dangerous reefs. Penhaligon cringed as the *Jagged Claw* sliced dangerously close to the razor-sharp coral, but Pig-wiggy, whether by luck or judgment, sailed the *Claw* safely to open water. Even under half sail, they picked up a fast pace around Howling Island. But Penhaligon could see that it was not fast enough for Mawgan.

"Now, Mawgan," he said, "it's your turn to trust me. If stony lunacrop is not the key ingredient, then what is?"

His father nodded. "I do trust you, Penhaligon, and you have a right to know about your heritage. Our serpent has an egg in her nest. We guess it is but a few weeks from hatching. It is a rare thing for a sea serpent to lay an egg. The shell is made from gold so valuable that treasure hunters and pirates spend their lives searching for such a prize."

"I understand that you must protect the egg, but how does that affect the survival of the Romany wolves?" asked Penhaligon.

Morgan lowered his voice as though spies were listening on the breeze. "The real value is that ground up to a powder, even a sprinkle of the golden shell is a wondrous healer. This is the key cure ingredient, not stony lunacrop. According to the elders, you cannot cure wolf fever without it."

Penhaligon thought of the page with the torn-off corner that had fallen from the book. Now it made sense. "A sprinkle of g—" "a sprinkle of golden serpent shell." In his hurry, he had ignored an ingredient in the cure, a terrible and presumptuous mistake for an apothecary.

"Our task of guarding the egg has been easy until now. No one ever sails near Howling Island. Many think it is haunted. The serpent entrusts the egg to us, especially when she is hunting for food." Mawgan grimaced. "I am worried that the wolves guarding the egg will be taken by surprise. They would not be expecting trouble."

"Then let's hope the reinforcements arrive in time," said Penhaligon. Mawgan didn't answer.

The object dropped by the serpent had now slid across the deck from its shadowy hiding place. Pig-wiggy picked it up and opened the container.

"Looks like a letter," he said, unfolding the paper that was inside. "Blimey! It's for you, Penhaligon."

"What's that, Pig-wiggy?" asked Penhaligon.

"The serpent dropped it. It's a message."

Penhaligon recognized the handwriting immediately and snatched the note from Pig-wiggy.

"Steady on . . . ," said Pig-wiggy. "You can ask nice, you know."

"Sorry, Pig-wiggy," said Penhaligon absentmindedly as he scanned the letter. He gasped.

"What is it?" asked Mawgan.

"A message from Rowan." Penhaligon passed him the note to read. "She says *febra lupi* has jumped species and that all creatures are now affected—half the village young ones. Mawgan, how is this possible?"

"I have no answer. But this is serious indeed."

"I need the eggshell and the stony lunacrop. We can fix this."

Mawgan shook his head. "It's too soon. The egg has not hatched. If you break the shell, the baby will die. And I believe this mother has laid her final egg. She is ages old, and perhaps the last of her kind. This egg must hatch or there will be no more."

It took Penhaligon only seconds to realize the problem: "And no way to cure future outbreaks of *febra lupi*." Penhaligon's brow furrowed deeply. "But, Mawgan, Donald and the young ones of Porthleven are sick now. They may not last until the egg hatches. How can we save them?"

Mawgan turned his shaggy head away. Penhaligon had his answer. There *was* no way to save them. His mind reeled at the thought.

🪶 🪶 🪶 🪶

"We're not going anywhere until that egg is in this boat!" shouted Dredge. He covered his ears with his paws. "And will you stop that racket?"

Elgato's purrs echoed around the cave like rumbling storm clouds. "Eet eez amazing," said Elgato. "No one eez believing this marvelous egg when I tell them."

"That's right! No one will believe it, because you're not going to tell a soul. Now jump up there on the ledge, both of you, and bring me the egg," Dredge hissed.

Hotchi gulped. "What if the serpent comes back? It will be right angry if it catches us stealing the egg."

"Well, you'd better hurry up then, hadn't you, Mister Spiny?" Dredge maneuvered the boat against the rock so Hotchi and Elgato could scramble over to the nest. The ledge was slick and slippery with green seaweed and scattered with withered plants that seemed to glow faintly in the dim light. The two creatures skidded along, holding on to each other for support. Elgato looked distastefully at the rickety serpent nest and carefully removed a piece of something that hung from one of the twigs in front of his nose.

Hotchi screwed up his snout. "Doesn't smell too good around here," he whispered.

"Eez probably *Capitán* Dredge," Elgato sniggered.

"I heard that!" roared Dredge. "Now get on with it. And don't drop the egg."

Elgato, being the taller of the two, climbed up the layers of old ships' timbers and branches and dropped himself into the nest. A soft layer of sand padded the inside, leaving room enough for a hatchling serpent to grow fat on tasty treats. The glowing egg highlighted the tips of Elgato's fur and his eyes shone like jewels. The thought of money caused the usual reaction in the cat.

"Stop purring!" ordered Dredge.

"I cannot help eet, I swear," cried Elgato. He tried to quiet himself and concentrated on picking up the egg. It was about the size of a large watermelon, and very heavy. No matter how he tried to grab it, the egg slipped through his paws. "Thees eez the most difficult egg!" he yowled.

"Roll it onto your jacket first," suggested Hotchi.

"Very smart, Mister 'Otchi," said Elgato. He took off his green velvet jacket and laid it in front of the egg.

"I roll a lot of 'erring barrels when I can't pick 'em up," said Hotchi, nervously searching the surrounding water with his sharp eyes. He had a bad feeling. The bow ferrets were guarding the entrance, but who knew what dangers were lurking beneath the black water? The serpent, after all, could swim unseen under their boat.

Just then, a low, growling snarl came from the dark shadows of the cave.

"What was that?" hissed Hotchi.

The shadows suddenly came alive. Out of nowhere, two loping figures sprang onto the ledge. Their eyes red and spittle flying from their fangs, they ran toward the hedgehog.

"Aaarrgh! Wolves!" Hotchi screamed, and scuttled up and into the nest like a squirrel.

"Fire!" Dredge ordered his bow ferrets.

A hail of arrows flew toward the ledge. The wolves darted behind some rocks, but an arrow found its target in one wolf's rump. A piercing howl echoed around the rocky cave, so loud that all had to cover their ears for fear of being deafened.

"Fire!" Dredge ordered again.

This time, most of the arrows fell short, landing with a clatter on the rock.

Then there was silence. No one moved.

"Bring . . . me . . . that . . . egg!" Dredge roared.

"B-b-but the wolves . . . ," whimpered Hotchi.

"They've gone, you fool. Listen . . . !"

Sure enough, they could hear distant howls from the mountain ridge above. Hotchi shivered. It was the first time he'd seen an actual full-grown Romany wolf, and he wondered if Donald would grow up to be that large.

"They are calling for help. If you two don't hurry, they'll be back . . . a whole pack of them," said Dredge.

"Eez good we hurry, Mister 'Otchi?"

"Right," said Hotchi, and after much huffing and puffing, the two of them had the egg wrapped in the jacket. Elgato tied the jacket arms to fashion a handle and climbed to the rim of the nest, pulling the egg behind him, with Hotchi pushing from the bottom. The hedgehog then climbed up and out of the nest, and Elgato lowered the egg down to his outstretched paws.

"Phew! It's heavy," panted Hotchi.

"If you drop it, I'll make mincemeat of you both!" Dredge yelled.

"He eez such a charming creature, no?" whispered Elgato.

Hotchi grinned in spite of himself, and between the two of them they coddled the egg to the rowboat, where

Dredge was rubbing his paws together.

"Well done, lads. Hand it over."

They had just passed the egg to Dredge when the ferret pointed behind them with a look of terror on his face. He shouted, "Oh no! The wolves!"

Elgato and Hotchi whipped around, expecting to see the ferocious shaggy creatures bearing down on them. But nothing was there.

"Dredge, no!" Elgato yelled. "Come back here! You cannot leave us."

Dredge had already rowed halfway to the entrance. "Ha! Your trick works well, Mister Spiny. Good-bye, Elgato," he laughed.

"Did you think I would take the chance of you blab-
bering to every creature in the Warped Board about
my golden egg?"

"I won't tell. I promeese," pleaded Elgato.

"That's right! You won't tell after that angry serpent has finished with you. Or maybe I should say
'finished you.' Or maybe the wolves will get here first.
Or maybe they'll all arrive at the same time! You can
make a bet with each other; you know how you like
to gamble, *Capitán* Furrari."

The bow ferrets started to cheer.

"Come on, lads," Dredge growled at the bow ferrets. "We don't want to be around when Mummy
arrives home!" Dredge patted the egg. "For the first
time in my miserable life, I am rich. When this baby
hatches, I will have a fortune in gold and my own
silver-scaled serpent. And I know just the place
where a baby silver-scaled serpent can grow up to
be a big, huge, enormous silver-scaled serpent . . .
where no one would think of looking." He laughed
triumphantly.

Hotchi and Elgato could still hear the cackling
laughter of Dredge and his ferrets long after the
boats had disappeared from view. They sat, miserable,
amongst the bony piles of leftovers.

"That eez what we weel look like soon," said Elgato, gloomily kicking at some fish spines.

"Not if we escape," said Hotchi.

"We could swim," said Elgato.

"Can't swim," said Hotchi.

"Me neither," Elgato sighed.

Hotchi raised his brows. "Let's look around the back of the cave: there's obviously another way out— the one the wolves used."

They searched the shadowy clefts of cold rock with their paws. But apart from squishy things that felt disgusting in the dark and some very sharp barnacles, they found nothing. It was hopeless.

"I'm going to miss my little 'uns," sniffed Hotchi. "And dear Mrs. Hotchi, my Heligan. I never did tell her 'ow much I appreciated the way she looked after me proper."

"Thees eez nice, Mister 'Otchi, that you have someone who will mees you." Elgato sighed. "I 'ave no one to mees me."

"There must be someone," said Hotchi.

Elgato thought for a moment. "There eez a feline once; Helen was her name. She had the most beautiful pink nose, and her smile . . . her smile, Mister 'Otchi, eez lighting this cave." He sighed. "I thought I was too young to settle. And so, eez as I say, no crea-ture, except maybe the landlord of the Warped Board. I weel mees my cowslip ale. Mmm . . . nice cool cowslip ale, I can almost taste eet, Mister 'Otchi."

"If we ever get out of this mess, Elgato, I'll buy you a barrelful."

Elgato laughed. "Mister 'Otchi, you are not so bad after all. You buy me a barrelful and I shall share eet with you . . . if we ever get out of this mess."

Just then, a long shadow fell across the mouth of the cave.

♟ ♟ ♟ ♟

Rowan held the lantern high so she could see her way along the musty-smelling passage. She recalled the time when Sir Derek had held her and Lady Ferball, his aunt, hostage at Ferball Manor. Back then, she had needed to travel unseen on her missions to the out-side, just like now.

The cobwebs were thick and dusty. The twins would have loved it. She felt a pang of sadness as she remembered how, just a few days ago, they were so excited about being chosen to lead the dance in the Ferball Festival. How quickly things could change.

The dust tickled her snout, and she was happy to

finally reach the descending steps that led to the greenhouse. She snuffed out the light before opening the greenhouse door. If the guards were still on the roof, they would see her lantern's glow through the glass panes. She gently slid open the panel and stepped into the thick ferns and Lady Ferball's prize aspidistras . . . so far, so good.

She crept from the greenhouse and saw that there was indeed a guard on the roof, but he had his back to her. The rain sheeted across the lawn, and Rowan was drenched within seconds as she ran across the grass and into the chestnut wood beyond. There were no shouts of discovery and no more guards. Now all she had to worry about was sneaking through the village to Rock Pool headland without being seen.

Rowan's fur was plastered to the side of her head, but she ignored the uncomfortable chill that crept up her back—the rain had its advantages. Most of the Royal Warthog Guard on quayside duty was keeping dry inside the Cat and Fiddle Public House. One long-suffering soldier, muttering to himself, was trying to shelter under the narrow porch of a fisherman's cottage. But Rowan knew that even one guard was enough to raise the alarm.

Hotchi's herring barrels were stacked on the dockside. She crept over to them with her half-sword and cut the ropes that bound them together. She pushed. Slowly, the barrels rolled toward the edge of the dock.

As they gathered speed, Rowan yelled out: "Help! Help!"

The barrels flew over the edge of the quay and hit the water with a splash.

"Who goes there?" The guard ran over to see who had fallen into the water. Rowan stole past him, smiling to herself.

Then she was heading up the steep hill toward Rock Pool Lighthouse. There were no warthogs in sight. Soon she would have her eggshells and be back at Ferball Manor in dry clothes, holding a cup of hot nettle tea . . . with extra honey.

The wind was fierce on the bleak headland, and she struggled through prickly gorse bushes to reach the red-and-white-striped lighthouse, whose lamp was already glowing in the faded evening light. Rowan made her way to the cliff edge, silently cursing the captain of the guard. If she had been able to get here earlier, she'd have had more daylight to complete her task.

The snake holes, she knew, were just over the edge

of the cliff, close to the place where she harvested the herbal plant swallowwort. In fear she would be blown over, she got down on her knees and crawled along the rim of the cliff. The ground was sodden, and dangerously unstable close to the edge: she drove her sword into the turf for an extra hold. Her new britches were covered in mud as she leaned over the cliff edge. She felt around for snake holes with her free arm. There was one right there, but she was not far enough over to reach inside. She wiped the dripping fur from her eyes and repositioned her half-sword.

"Just a little bit further . . . ," she groaned, stretching her body to the full. She felt the dirt at the cliff edge give way, she was so close . . . almost there. But the ground collapsed again, this time breaking away in a large muddy clod. She tumbled over the edge, hanging on to her half-sword for dear life.

🦔 🦔 🦔 🦔

Pig-wiggy's Mohawk ruffled in the breeze as he steered the *Jagged Claw* around the island.

"He's a fine captain, for a guinea pig," Mawgan said as the pig shouted orders to his crew of two.

"It's all he ever wanted to do, he says. We're lucky Dredge left him behind," said Penhaligon.

Mawgan laughed. "Penhaligon, tell me more about my father," he said.

"Menhenin was a fine apothecary," began Penhaligon, and as the wind filled the sails, Penhaligon resolved to lighten the mood. He told tales that made his father howl with laughter. How Menhenin scolded Penhaligon for putting the classroom bullies to sleep with sleeping potion, and Menhenin's stories of grateful Uvian princes sending him flowing robes and turbans that he would wear even on the hottest days, to disguise his real identity as a Romany wolf.

"He was like the father I never had," said Penhaligon. And then he suddenly realized what he had said. "I'm sorry, Mawgan, I didn't mean . . ."

"It's the truth, Penhaligon, however much it hurts." Mawgan's eyes filled with sorrow. "How did he die?"

It was true, and the truth did sometimes hurt. Penhaligon knew that he would have to tell Mawgan about the Purple Moor tribe. "You told me that the elders were worried that a catastrophe would befall the wolves. I have to tell you that that is exactly what happened. I do not have all the answers. All I know is that the tribe was wiped out by wolf fever. Menhenin caught it too, though at the time I did not know what it was."

Mawgan gasped. "All of them?"

"Except for Donald and Dora, but now, as you know, their lives hang in the balance."

"It is a curse indeed." Mawgan remained silent until the towering cliffs of Serpent Ridge came into view.

"I can't see the *Shriek*!" called Pig-wiggy.

There was no sign of the *Black Shriek*, not even on the horizon. It was too much to hope that Dredge had changed his mind and sailed elsewhere. Had he left already? Had he found what he was looking for? They needed to check the serpent nest. Pig-wiggy sailed as close as he dared to the cliff face and they dropped anchor. Penhaligon and Mawgan rowed to the hidden cave entrance.

"I can see why no one has ever discovered the serpent's lair," said Penhaligon.

Mawgan sighed. "The creature will need a new hiding place from now on . . . if it has survived Dredge's bow ferrets."

A sudden screaming wail filled the air. Penhaligon had never heard anything like it. It came from inside the cave.

"Quickly," said Mawgan. "That's the serpent."

They rowed into the cave, to a sight Penhaligon would never forget. Scattered across the ledge was a jumble of fish skeletons and wood, the remains of the serpent's nest. There, in the middle of the mess, reared up to her full height, was the serpent. And screaming for all they were worth were Hotchi and Elgato, sticking out of her jaws.

R owan dared not move. The sword was holding, but she knew that it might slip out of the wet ground without warning. Below her she could see the sharp rocks of Rock Pool Cliff.

"Falling is not an option. Concentrate!" she told herself. "Donald needs me." Her thoughts were racing. She closed her eyes and took a deep breath.

When she opened her eyes, she caught sight of the rough seas pounding the Spatavian wreck. She and Penhaligon had been so brave that night so many seasons ago. Now she must be brave again.

She turned her gaze upward. There were two snake holes right in front of her, and one of them had many shell halves tucked inside; there didn't even seem to be a snake to chase away.

"What luck!" she said to herself, and then realized

what a ridiculous thing that was to say when one was hanging from a cliff.

Just to her right, a piece of rock stuck out from the cliff face. If she could just reach it with her hind leg, she might be able to take some weight off the sword. She flung out her leg, but her britches caught on a branch growing out from the cliff face. Rowan yanked free and heard a tearing noise. "Darn!" she muttered, wondering how big of a rip she'd made.

Gingerly, she tried again. She felt for the rock and placed a little weight on it. It held firm. After twisting herself around, she managed to find another hold. She pressed against the side of the cliff, where the rain funneled down in muddy rivulets. Carefully, she took one paw off the sword handle and slowly reached inside the snake hole.

"Please let there be no snakes," she said under her breath, feeling around for some already hatched shells. Touching something long and smooth, she yelped and snatched out her paw. But no snake came slithering out, as they usually did when disturbed. She peered inside the hole and saw some kind of package. Again she reached inside and pulled out a ragged pouch wrapped with string. She tucked it into the waistband of her britches and then collected several snake-egg shells and stuffed them, crumbling, into her pocket. She sighed with relief. Now all she had to do was climb back up the cliff.

Holding tight to a rock with one paw, she pulled the sword from the turf with the other and inched sideways to find firmer ground, working her way across the cliff face. At last she found a firm ledge where she could climb more easily to the cliff top. This was probably the way Donald would have come.

"Donald," she breathed, and with a last burst of energy, flopped her body over the top of the cliff. She lay there, exhausted. Every muscle twitched. After a few minutes, she sat up and examined the pouch she'd found in the snake hole. It was grubby but quite dry, and Rowan gently undid it. She smiled at her discovered treasure. Inside were a slingshot, some marbles, and a compass that Penhaligon had given Donald for his birthday. But the smile left her face when she saw something else: a rag wolf doll with a face of clay and wearing tattered clothes singed from fire. Rowan gasped as she recognized the doll from Donald's past life with the Romany wolves. All the cubs' clothes and possessions were supposed to have been destroyed in case they were contaminated by the fever. Donald must have rescued his doll from the fire and kept it hidden all this time. Had he caught wolf fever from this?

Rowan did not care if she was heard or not. She threw the doll over the cliff with all her might, tossed back her head, and howled in despair.

"Flaming foxgloves!" yelled Penhaligon as he saw Hotchi and Elgato sticking out from the sea serpent's jaws.

"Quick! Row closer. She is very upset," said Mawgan.

"Upset! Mawgan, she's going to eat them," said Penhaligon, horrified.

"Serpents only eat fish, luckily. But she may crunch on them a little bit."

Penhaligon rowed faster. He could feel the serpent's distress at losing her egg. She moaned while Hotchi and Elgato pleaded for help.

"It thinks we stole the egg. Tell it we didn't steal

the egg!" shrieked Hotchi.

"There is only one thing that will calm her," said Mawgan. He started to hum the lullaby that was now familiar to Penhaligon. When Penhaligon joined in, Mawgan said, "Louder!"

The two of them sang at the top of their lungs, above the lamenting wails of the sea serpent and her victims. As the tune reached her ears, she stopped moaning but did not let go of Hotchi and Elgato. She swayed her head back and forth to the music.

"Whoa! Stop! I feeling seasick!" yelled Elgato.

The serpent suddenly spat out Elgato and Hotchi as though they were a couple of rotten fish. They landed, with a splash, in the water.

"Help!" they shouted.

"Oh no! Hotchi can't swim," said Penhaligon. He saw Elgato splashing desperately in the water. "And neither can Elgato, it looks like."

"Go rescue them," said Mawgan. "I need to calm the serpent." Then Mawgan dove into the water and, in a few smooth, strong strokes, reached the rocky ledge.

Penhaligon realized from whom he had inherited his swimming ability as he rowed to the floundering Elgato and Hotchi. He pulled them into the boat.

"Penhaligon! You saved us," said Hotchi, whose spines were so pale they were almost colorless.

Elgato, for once, had nothing to say as he sat shivering in the boat. The three of them watched Mawgan speak softly and stroke the serpent. When he finally signaled that it was safe for them to join him, Penhaligon rowed to the ledge. They saw milky-colored tears rolling from her eyes. Penhaligon felt an overwhelming sadness. The egg was a great loss for all of them—it was so important, for so many reasons, for so many creatures.

"It not be our fault, Penhaligon," said Hotchi. "It's Dredge that took the egg. Then 'e abandoned us 'ere."

"Do you know where he took it?" asked Mawgan.

Hotchi gawped at Mawgan, wide-eyed, as he realized, for the first time, that he was in the presence of a large, unknown wolf and that it had just asked him a question.

Penhaligon couldn't help but smile. "Don't worry, Hotchi. Allow me to introduce my father, Mawgan, chief of the Howling Island wolf tribe.

"N-n-nice to meet you," Hotchi said in a hoarse whisper. "Penhaligon, I thought you was an orphan."

"It's a long story, Hotchi. Do you know where Dredge has gone?"

" 'E just said that 'e knew a place where 'e could raise a baby serpent," said Hotchi.

"Eez a place where no one would think, he say," added Elgato, trying to keep his distance from both the serpent and Mawgan.

"Any idea where that might be, Penhaligon?" Mawgan asked.

"Perhaps," said Penhaligon. "I need to ask Pigwiggy."

"Then we must make haste back to the ship," said Mawgan. "Maybe we can catch the *Black Shriek*."

"Yes," said Penhaligon, "but before I leave the island, we must harvest the stony lunacrop."

Mawgan nodded. "We must be quick, my son. You two stay here with the serpent. Take care of her," he told Hotchi and Elgato.

The gray cat sat at the very edge of the ledge, as far from the serpent as possible, and watched Mawgan and Penhaligon disappear into the shadows at the rear of the cave. He looked at Hotchi in disbelief.

"So, Mister 'Otchi, there *was* another way out," he said. We need not have suffered such indignities by this creature." He pointed accusingly at the serpent, who rested her head in what was left of her nest.

Hotchi gingerly patted the serpent's nose. She sniffed, and another tear ran down her silver scales. "At least she didn't crunch us," he said.

♻ ♻ ♻ ♻

Penhaligon followed Mawgan up the rough-hewn steps that led to Serpent Ridge. The evening was fresh and crisp when they emerged from the passage, and a sweet smell lingered in the air. A dark mass of forest stretched beneath them on one side of the ridge, the ocean on the other.

Mawgan looked at the night sky. Only one or two stars twinkled above. "The moon is veiled by clouds. Stony lunacrop can only be picked under the light of the moon. We will have to wait."

Penhaligon remembered the cryptic clues written on the recipe. "By the light of the moon"—yes, he remembered reading that with Gertrude. It all seemed so long ago. He took a seat on a boulder and looked out to sea. The *Jagged Claw* was at anchor in the calm water, and he wondered how Dora was feeling.

Mawgan sat next to him. "While we wait for the moon to shine, will you tell me more, Penhaligon?" he asked.

And so Penhaligon told of his childhood with the Brock family, his apprenticeship with Menhenin, and how he had inherited the apothecary in Ramble-on-the-Water after Menhenin had died of *febra lupi*.

"I wish I had known he was my grandfather," he said sadly.

"Would you have loved him more?" asked Mawgan.

Penhaligon smiled and shook his head. "No, probably not."

"I know he would have been proud of you, just as I am," said Mawgan.

"Proud? But I have failed. My fox-mate, Rowan,

trusted me to find the cure to save Donald. We have lost the egg. I have only enough cure for one creature, and possibly the whole village is sick by now."

"Your mother believed in me too, Penhaligon," said Mawgan. "I thought I could solve everything if we could find a new beginning. I learned, too late, that sometimes it is better to try and make the best of what you already have. Rowan loves you. She will know you tried your best."

"She will lose everything she holds dear if I cannot find the egg, Mawgan. And so will I."

"We will find it," said Mawgan.

"We? How can you come with me?" asked Penhaligon. "Suppose you catch wolf fever?"

"I'll take my chances," said Mawgan. "I am the chief of this tribe, and it's up to me to protect the serpent and her egg."

"But suppose we can't catch Dredge? You will have exposed yourself to the fever when all hope for cure is lost—you could return here and infect the whole tribe. You have to protect them also."

The cry of wolves howled across the ridge. Reinforcements were almost there, but alas, too late.

Mawgan bowed his head. "Things happen to mold our lives without us realizing it, Penhaligon." He sighed. "If I cannot come with you, then you must find the golden egg and return it here."

Penhaligon turned to his father. "I need it for the cure, Mawgan. How can I let the cubs and possibly all the young ones of the village die?"

"You must not use the shell before the egg has hatched! If you do, there will be no more serpents and no more eggs—ever."

Now it was Penhaligon's turn to sigh and bow his head. What an impossible choice!

"You will decide what is right at the right time, Penhaligon. I have no doubt."

Just then, the newly risen creamy white moon peeked out from behind the clouds. Penhaligon watched

in wonder as the ground around them lit up with thousands of tiny glowing flower heads.

"Behold," said Mawgan. "Stony lunacrop."

🕯 🕯 🕯 🕯

The stony lunacrop was harvested and the *Jagged Claw* was ready to leave just as the moon reached its highest point in the sky. Penhaligon had been right: Pigwiggy did have an idea where Dredge was headed.

"Cap'n Dredge was always muttering about the same creature you was asking about, Penhaligon. Inherited a castle in the north, 'e did, with a lake an' everythin'. Derek, the galley cat."

Penhaligon grinned. Lady Ferball would have loved to hear her nephew, the evil Sir Derek, referred to as a galley cat.

"Then that is where we must go," said Penhaligon.

The plan was to harness the serpent in order to tow the *Jagged Claw* back to Porthleven. There, they would leave Dora so that she could be taken care of properly in Ferball Hospital. With serpent power and the wind behind them, the journey would be quick— perhaps they would even catch up with the *Black Shriek*. From Porthleven they would head north toward Sir Derek's castle. Mawgan told them the serpent would sense her egg when she was close enough. "Then she will tell you where to go," he said.

"Tell me? Like an uninvited thought?" asked Penhaligon. "She will show me the place."

Mawgan laughed. "So she's been talking to you already? You'd better watch out, Penhaligon." Mawgan slapped him on the back. "You'll end up being a Keeper."

A loop of rope was tied to the bow of the ship while Mawgan "spoke" with the serpent. She happily took up the rope in her jaws, ready to speed them along their way.

Mawgan hugged Penhaligon. "I feel as if I am losing you again," he said sadly.

Penhaligon swallowed hard. "We will see each other again soon."

Mawgan rowed into the dark night, back to Howling Island. As the *Jagged Claw* sailed away, Penhaligon imagined him waving from Serpent Ridge, bathed in moonlight and surrounded by a thousand sparkling stars. He raised his paw. "Good-bye, Father," he said.

Ferrets at the Gate

S ir Derek licked his lips as he slid the last siz-zling fish, dripping with butter, onto the serv-ing platter, then made his way to the dining room. He had already set the banquet table with his plate and some bread. He did not care that he was the only one sitting at the long table that had enough room for twelve felines. He liked living in the castle on his own.

It was very inconvenient that his servant, who was quite sick with a fever, had to go home early, but Sir Derek did not want to take the chance of catching anything from one of the common creatures from the nearby village.

The mouthwatering fish had been caught in the loch just that morning and was so fresh he knew that it would almost melt in his mouth. The loch, which stretched in front of his castle, was fed by a mountain stream at one end and ran out to the sea at the other. This salt- and freshwater mix gave the fish a sublime taste, and Sir Derek never tired of having fish for dinner day after day.

He sat down quickly. His feast would soon go cold in the drafty old castle. His mother had never been one to spend money on repairs, and Derek was not about to spend his either. Not that she'd left him much. He'd only inherited the castle because none of his brothers or sisters wanted it.

He tucked a napkin into his collar, picked up his fork, and was about to spear a fish from the platter when he heard a loud pounding on the castle door. Sir Derek ignored it. But the banging continued. It sounded like whoever it was, was using a battering ram.

"Go away!" he yelled.

But the noise grew louder. Derek threw down his fork and his napkin and hurried angrily to the door. He opened it with such force that the ferrets who tumbled in almost landed on top of him.

"Good evening, *Sir* Derek," said Captain Dredge, standing in the doorway. His voice was as crisp as a hard frost.

"What the . . . ? What are you doing here?"

demanded Derek, screwing his nose up at the heap of smelly ferrets at his feet.

"You left my ship with a small unpaid debt. So here I am to collect it." Dredge pushed past Derek, into the castle hallway. "Mummy saw you right, I see," he said, glancing around. "Could do with a little something here and there."

"I d-don't have any m-money," stammered Sir Derek.

"Oh, I don't need your money," said Dredge. "Just your noble hospitality."

Derek looked confused.

"It's been a long, hard sail from Howling Island, and me and my crew are tired." Dredge sniffed the air. "And hungry. We shall be living here for a while."

"But my castle . . . your ferrets," Sir Derek sputtered. "They are so . . . dirty and messy and . . . stinky." He noticed what looked to be a large egg wrapped in a velvet jacket under Dredge's arm. "What's that?"

"Ah yes," said Dredge. "This shall live here too; in the loch, to be more precise."

"What is it?" Derek tried to look inside.

"A sea-serpent egg."

"No!" Derek took a step back. "You can't—not a sea serpent! Not in my loch! They are supposed to do nothing but eat fish. It'll clean me out. I won't stand for it!" he said.

Dredge laughed. Then his grin disappeared. He leaned in only a few inches from Derek's face. Sir Derek held his breath so as not to breathe in the ferret's offensive odor.

"You," said Dredge, "will do as you're told. You owe me. In a season or two, the thing will be big enough for me to slaughter and sell its silver scales."

"A *season* or two?" Derek felt as though he would faint.

"If you stop whining, I might give you a couple of scales for your trouble." Dredge looked around. "You can get the place fixed up." Then he walked into the dining room and called to his crew. "Sit down, lads," he said. "The galley cat is just about to cook us up some more fish—aren't you, Pussface?"

The ferrets pushed and shoved one another to scoop up the fish on the serving platter and started to holler for more. Sir Derek could not believe his rotten luck: once again he was a galley slave to a band of ill-mannered, uncultured hooligan ferrets.

🕯 🕯 🕯 🕯

When she finally found herself back in the greenhouse, Rowan was smeared from head to hind in mud, her britches torn beyond repair. The rain had helped her dodge the guards on her mission, but she knew she should change from her wet clothes quickly. She already felt feverish.

She closed the secret door behind her. Her paws were shaking so much that she could barely light the lantern. The dark passage had never seemed so long as she dragged herself up the steep steps. She pushed through the secret door of the bedroom with her last ounce of strength.

"Rowan! Whatever has happened?" Gertrude ran over to Rowan just as she collapsed. "Bancroft, come quick! I've found her."

Bancroft came hurrying into the bedroom. "Oh my goodness, look at the state! Rowan, you look like a mud monster."

Rowan smiled weakly as they helped her over to a chair. "How's Donald?" she asked.

"Bancroft, make up the fire, would you? She's freezing," said Gertrude.

"How's Donald?" she asked again.

"I think the poison has started to spread," Gertrude said quietly. "He has the cough."

Before long, a fire was roaring in the grate. Bancroft hurried to make some nettle tea while Gertrude tried to put Rowan to bed.

"Come on, Rowan, you're very sick."

"No!" insisted Rowan. "I must make the cure, for Donald." She pulled out the snake shells.

"You're in no fit state to make anything," said Gertrude.

"But . . . he'll die."

"I'll prepare the cure," said Gertrude. "But—only after you get into bed."

Rowan nodded her agreement.

After Gertrude had taken off Rowan's muddy clothes and helped her into a warm nightgown, she headed down to the dungeon, stopping first in the library for the page of cure ingredients she and Penhaligon had first found in the book. It seemed like an age ago.

The dungeon was cold and creepy. She'd never liked it down there, so she would gather her ingredients quickly. She read through the cure, putting each herb in turn into a basket. Thankfully, Rowan and Penhaligon used the same alphabetical system that she did, and in a very short time, she had everything she needed except for the stony lunacrop. Finally she placed the stone mortar and pestle into the basket. She hurried back up the steps, happy to leave the spooky dungeon behind.

Rowan was waiting for her, too weak to get out of bed.

"I have everything," said Gertrude. "By the way, you should get that sea-hole cover fixed. That could be dangerous."

Rowan managed a weak smile. She prayed that the snake shells might make a difference. What did they have to lose? Gertrude pummeled and ground the herbs and snake shells, carefully adding the oils. She did everything perfectly.

Gertrude looked at Rowan. "Everything," she said, "except the stony lunacrop."

Rowan gazed into the heart of the fire as if searching for a sign. "It's coming," said Rowan. "He won't let me down."

The *Jagged Claw* creaked and rolled as the serpent sped across the seas toward Penhaligon's homeland.

"I'm not sure if this old boat can handle the strain," said Hotchi.

"She eez fine," said Elgato, indignant. But he

muttered something in Spatavian under his breath, and Penhaligon smiled as he saw Elgato cross his paws together. Penhaligon left Elgato, Hotchi, and Pig-wiggy on deck while he went to check on Dora. Her condition had steadily become worse, and Penhaligon had not been able to control her fever. He opened the door quietly.

"Dora, how are you feeling?" There was no answer. Penhaligon hoped that she was sleeping, and he tiptoed over. He gasped when he saw her. She lay staring at nothing, her eyes clouded over. "Oh no!" he cried.

The cub's fever was so high that her fur was dripping wet all over. He tried to cool her with compresses of seawater. Nothing helped. He felt the vial of cure in his pocket. He took it out and studied it. Maybe if he just used half, as she'd only just started with the disease . . . then maybe if he added more stony lunacrop to the remaining mixture for Donald? But what if half was not enough to cure either Dora or Donald? He looked at the young cub. He remembered all the times they'd played on the beach together, the long walks over the hills, and the hugs they'd shared. The little family he'd found, he was slowly losing. He did not have the golden egg, and he couldn't be certain they would find it at all, let alone in time to save anyone.

Just then, Dora's lower jaw fell open. Her usually pink tongue fell out to the side, dry and white. Without another thought, Penhaligon held open her snout and poured in all the mixture.

🐾 🐾 🐾 🐾

The crew of the *Jagged Claw,* such as it was, cheered when they saw the flashing beacon light of Rock Pool Lighthouse. The serpent had towed them so quickly that the poor ship had sprung small leaks all over its hull. They felt sure that the *Black Shriek* could be only a few hours ahead of them.

They would anchor off Brigand's Point, as Porthleven Harbor was way too shallow for such a large vessel. After they had taken Dora to Ferball Manor, they would use Hotchi's fishing boat to travel north to find Derek's castle. This was safer, said Penhaligon, as Dredge would not recognize the vessel.

"Besides," said Hotchi with less tact, "the *Claw* would never make it one mile further." Even Elgato couldn't deny this.

Penhaligon was not sure how to tell the serpent

this plan, but he decided he should sing the Romany lullaby first and see what happened. He pictured the *Claw* at anchor at Brigand's Point and then Hotchi's fishing boat, tied up at Porthleven quay. The serpent dropped the rope from her mouth and rolled in the surf before disappearing under the waves.

"I hope you got that. Um . . . thank you!" called Penhaligon over the side of the ship. The others stared at him as though he had been drinking seawater.

The moon was covered by storm clouds as they anchored the ship, and the whole crew rowed to shore on a pitch-black sea. Penhaligon noticed that the lights of the quay were brighter than usual.

"What's going on over there?" he said. "Can anyone see that far?"

Elgato squinted up his cat eyes. "Eet eez a lot of fire beacons along the quay. Eet eez a lot of soldiers too, wearing helmets with tusk things," he said, using his paws to show where the "tusk things" were.

Penhaligon whistled under his breath. "The Royal Warthog Guard," he said. "They must be here to stop creatures from leaving the village and spreading *febra lupi*."

"What about creatures wishing to come in?" asked Elgato.

Penhaligon sighed. "This may be more difficult than we thought."

They rowed in silence until they reached the shore, and pulled the rowboat onto the beach at Sandy Cove.

"We'll climb the steps up to Brigand's Point," said Penhaligon, "Follow me, and don't make a sound."

It was hard going with Dora flopped over Penhaligon's shoulder, but with Elgato's help they made it up to the flat, scrubby ground of Brigand's Point. There were few trees there and the winds blew hard across the open land.

But luck was with them, and they did not see any guards until they were close to Ferball Manor. Penhaligon signaled for everyone to follow him. He crept through the chestnut wood around the back of the house, grateful that the night was so dark. Soon they were at the edge of the wood, looking out over the Ferball Manor lawn. Penhaligon gazed at the large bay window of Rowan's bedroom. The glow from the hearth flickered shadows across the ceiling.

"Up there, on the roof, there will be guards," whispered Penhaligon. "Stay here and wait for me. I will deliver Dora and the stony lunacrop to Rowan. Then I'll be right back."

The others nodded in agreement. Penhaligon carefully made his way to the greenhouse. Quietly closing the door behind him, he pushed though the aspidistras and ferns by the back wall. Dora was sleeping peacefully, and he laid her gently on the greenhouse floor while he slid open the secret door. He sniffed the air. He smelled the sulfurous tang of a matchstick. Someone had been here recently. He found a lantern, but no matches. How would he be able to see in the tunnel? This was a blow.

Just then, a weak beam of moonlight shone through the glass greenhouse roof. Penhaligon had an idea. He pulled out a handful of stony lunacrop from the pouch. The tiny flower heads glowed silver as they fed on the light. There must be a metallic mineral in this herb, he thought. No wonder the serpent eats it to keep its scales healthy. When the flowers were quite bright, he tipped them into the lantern. They shone just enough in the dark tunnel that he could see his way, but he would have to be quick. He scooped up Dora and hurried along the passage, up the steps, and to the secret door leading into the bedroom. He burst into the room.

"Penhaligon!" screamed Gertrude. "You scared the life out of me!"

"Sorry, Gertrude."

Rowan opened her eyes at the sound of Penhaligon's voice. "Penhaligon?" she said weakly.

Penhaligon lay Dora down on the couch, and Gertrude covered her with a blanket.

"Rowan," said Penhaligon, going to her bedside. "My dearest. I wasn't sure if I would ever see you again." He kissed her paw and held it to his cheek.

"Penhaligon, you're here."

"Shh!" he said gently. "Rowan, I have so much to tell you." He stroked her ears and was shocked to feel the telltale lumps. He looked at Gertrude. There was nothing to say.

"I've brought your naughty cub back," he continued. "She's lying on the couch by the fire. She's fast asleep and is going to be just fine. And look,"

he said, holding up the lantern, where the stony lunacrop still glowed. "Isn't it beautiful?"

Rowan smiled. "I knew you'd find it," she said as she drifted off into feverish sleep.

Penhaligon stood up and whispered to Gertrude, "How's Donald?"

Gertrude shook her head. "Not good, Penhaligon. The cough has started. He's very weak. Rowan had me make up this cure with the snake shells she collected. She went to the cliff in the storm. She has a nasty fever."

"I don't think the snake shell will work, Gertrude. It is serpent shell we need."

Gertrude sat down. "Wherever can we get serpent shell at this time of night . . . or any other time, for that matter?"

"I have an idea where," said Penhaligon gruffly. "I must leave now to find it. Here is some stony lunacrop. Mix it with the potion while the flowers are still glowing; perhaps it will help ease their discomfort. I will return as soon as I can." He looked at Rowan, her fur still matted with mud, one last time before slipping into the secret passage.

The others were waiting in the chestnut wood. Penhaligon said nothing, but strode past them.

"What eez up with the fox?" Elgato asked Hotchi.

Hotchi had never seen Penhaligon behave in such a way. "I'm not sure I want to know," he said, and scurried after his friend.

Penhaligon kept up his fast pace, and the others hurried behind in fear of losing him. They kept within the thick of the trees as far as they could, until they reached the village outskirts. Now that the rain had stopped, several guards were warming themselves next to small bonfires they'd set along the quayside.

"Which boat eez yours, Mister 'Otchi?" asked Elgato.

Hotchi pointed proudly to his neat blue fishing boat, moored alongside the dock.

"Eet eez very nice," said the cat.

"Blimey," said Pig-wiggy. "How do we get over there without being seen?"

"There is no way without being seen," said Penhaligon. "We will have to make a run for it, and maybe fight our way through."

Hotchi gulped. "But they are the Royal Guard. They'll make pickled 'erring out of us."

"Whatever happens, my friends, the golden egg must be found without fail," said Penhaligon. He thought for a moment. "Here's the plan. I shall confront the guards and then lead them away through the narrow streets. While they are chasing me, you three run to the boat."

"But we need you, Penhaligon," said Hotchi.

"You don't need me to sail your boat, and Elgato and Pig-wiggy will help you rescue the egg."

"He eez right, Penhaligon, we do need you," said Elgato. "I will do the running through the village."

"No!" squeaked Pig-wiggy. "We need that serpent to scare the britches off the guards, that's who we need."

"I'll try to reach her, but I can't be sure she'll hear. I don't know where she is," said Penhaligon.

"Well, let me distract the guards, Mr. Penhaligon. You'll be more 'elp rescuing the egg. I'm good at running. Watch this!" The other three looked at Pig-wiggy's dancing feet as his orange Mohawk bobbed up and down. Pig-wiggy looked up at his three companions. "I am, really."

Penhaligon slapped him on the back. "Come on," he said, "let's just all make a run for it! If two of us can get through, it'll have to be enough. After three. One . . . two . . ."

Before Penhaligon had reached the third count, Elgato jumped up and ran yowling into the square, his sword brandished, his fur flying. The warthogs were so surprised, they just stood there, watching him.

"Well, come *on!*" spat Elgato, his paw on his hip. "You rotund, hairy beasts with large protruding teeths!"

The warthogs grunted and moved toward Elgato. The cat started to run, but they tackled him before he had made it halfway across the quayside. Penhaligon winced, knowing that Elgato was somewhere on the bottom of the heavy pile.

"Come on," he said, and the three companions raced for Hotchi's boat. They had almost made it when more of the guard came running out of the Cat and Fiddle.

"After them!" yelled their captain.

Penhaligon ran as fast as he could. Then he heard Hotchi's cries. "Flaming foxgloves!" he muttered, turning back and jumping on the guards who had Hotchi by the arms.

Squealing away, Pig-wiggy ran in between the soldiers' legs, tripping them up and biting as many as he could about the ankles with his sharp front teeth.

There was such a commotion that villagers poked their heads out their cottage windows.

"Look! It's Penhaligon," shouted one.

"Penhaligon's back!" shouted Bill Goat. "Everybody, let's help him. They can't catch all of us!"

Doors were flung open all around the square, and the cobblestoned quay was suddenly mobbed with villagers running this way and that. There had never been such uproar in Porthleven. The Royal Warthog Guard frantically tried to catch the curfew breakers. Bill Goat stood on a table outside the Cat and Fiddle and, using his walking stick, knocked the visors on the guards' helmets closed so that they couldn't see where they were going.

"Take that!" he bleated. "And that, and that, and that!"

The fiddlers and drummers struck up a fast, merry tune to help along the spirit of the free-for-all. It was the most fun the villagers had had in ages.

Penhaligon closed his eyes and concentrated as hard as he could.

"What are ye doing?" shouted Hotchi. "This is no time to daydream, Penhaligon."

"Right! Let's go, Hotchi." And amidst the confusion, the fox and his band of cohorts made a run to the fishing boat. Hotchi cast off the lines and jumped on board behind Penhaligon and Pig-wiggy, but the

boat started to move before Hotchi had even hoisted the sail. He looked at Penhaligon, puzzled.

"It pays to have friends." The fox grinned.

Hotchi saw the flash of silver through the dark water and laughed. "This be a grand adventure now, Penhaligon."

Pig-wiggy gave a shout. "Look! It's Elgato!"

Penhaligon saw the cat crawl out from under the pile of warthog guards. Then he was running for all he was worth toward Hotchi's boat as it drifted away from the side of the dock.

"Mister 'Otchi, wait for me!" he yowled.

The guards were almost upon Elgato once again. The sea serpent suddenly reared up and sprayed the screaming warthogs with water as she dropped a sodden item at Penhaligon's feet.

"Aaaarrgh!" the guards and the villagers cried. "Monsters!" And they all scrambled quickly in the opposite direction.

"Jump, Elgato! Jump!" cried Hotchi.

Elgato flew through the air, his body stretched in a sleek arc. He landed on the deck with inches to spare.

"Impressive!" said Penhaligon.

"I am not the Elgato for nothing," said the cat. He purred.

"Elgato," said Hotchi. "You be purrin', and no one 'as so much as mentioned money."

Elgato smiled. "A good fight, a hopeless cause, brave companions . . . thees is reeches, I think, Mister 'Otchi," he said.

A fading moon painted a faint silver path for them across the ocean. The sea serpent pushed Hotchi's boat far beyond Porthleven Bay, and the hedgehog steered a northerly course, heading for the brightest star before it vanished with the approaching dawn. Penhaligon examined the squishy mess that the serpent had dropped.

It was a slipper.

"I'd recognize those pom-poms anywhere," he laughed. "We must be close," he told the others. "This"—he waved the bedraggled shoe in the air—"is Sir Derek's slipper."

Elgato raised his brow. "What kind of creature eez wearing slippers such as these?"

"Only a puffed-up cat like Sir Derek," said Penhaligon. "But it appears our serpent has found the castle *and* a way into it."

The boat made speedy progress northward and Hotchi broke out Heligan Hotchi-witchi's apple cake, a tin of which he always kept on board. Washed down with blackberry ale, it was as good as a feast.

Penhaligon saw the familiar cliffs of his home replaced by an unyielding mountainous shoreline. All was quiet save the swoosh of water against the hull and the occasional snap of the sail as it ballooned in the breeze. He was lucky to have these companions. None of them had needed to come, to put themselves in danger, but they had anyway, without a question. He smiled and watched them. Elgato, standing proud on the bow—a cat down on his luck who had put bravery before fortune. Pig-wiggy, whose dreams were so much bigger than his own self. And Hotchi, dear Hotchi. Salt of the earth—a more solid and true friend you couldn't wish for.

Elgato pointed toward the shoreline. "I think we are here, Mister 'Otchi. Look!"

They saw an estuary, a dark, wide river that flowed from between the mountains. The river led inland toward some hills, and they could just make out the shape of a large dwelling on the left side of a valley.

The tiller swung sharply, and Hotchi's boat turned itself toward the shore. They lowered the sail. They would stand no chance against the ferrets if they were seen or heard. Surprise was their only ally. The serpent pulled them farther up the narrowing river.

"Look over there," whispered Pig-wiggy. "It's the *Black Shriek.*"

The ferrets had made a poor attempt to hide their ship in an overgrown part of the riverbank. "They probably couldn't get any further up the river," Pig-wiggy said. "I expect we'll be smellin' 'em mighty soon."

The river led to an enormous body of water—a loch that stretched its long finger up into the valley. Penhaligon thought it the loneliest-looking place he'd ever seen.

The serpent gave Hotchi's boat a final nudge into the loch and disappeared under the water. The companions looked to shore, where a towering castle stood on the bank. Everyone's heart sank. It was a fortress.

"How do we get in?" asked Hotchi. "We can 'ardly knock at the front door."

"Where *is* the front door?" asked Pig-wiggy.

Penhaligon stared at Sir Derek's castle without saying a word. In his mind he could see the image of some type of cellar. Two boats were moored against a wide stone ledge. He saw the mate to Derek's slipper sitting by one of them. He knew the serpent was talking to him, but he could not understand what she meant.

"We have to sneak in," he said. "Dredge will not be expecting us—he thinks that I'm a castaway on Howling Island, Hotchi and Elgato are serpent snacks, and Pig-wiggy is still sitting in the *Jagged Claw*, anchored off Howling Bay."

Elgato studied the castle through Hotchi's spyglass. The walls were of sheer stone, the high, narrow windows barred with iron grilles. The lakeside wall rose out of the loch itself, with high turreted towers at each end of the ramparts. At the base of the wall, water lapped under an archway just large enough for a rowboat. That too was blocked, by a portcullis of iron bars.

"So where will this sneaking take place?" asked Elgato. "I don't even see any door. They do not welcome the guests here."

"In my experience," said Pig-wiggy, "these rich, lordy types always 'ave a way out, just in case they's ever have to do a bunk quick-like. All we have to do is find it and creep in . . ." The other three looked at him, mystified. "An escape route," Pig-wiggy explained.

Hotchi looked at the thick, gorse-covered mountain slope. "Could be anywhere," he said. "If there is one. Would we find it?"

They all sighed.

Just then, the serpent draped her long neck over the side of the boat, showering them with cold water.

"Hey! Watch out; that's freezing," complained Hotchi, shaking the water from his spiny head.

Penhaligon scratched the serpent behind her gills. "Well-done," he said when he saw the image in his head. "She has shown me the underwater way in."

"That's no good to us," said Pig-wiggy. "Hotchi and Elgato can't even swim."

"The serpent will take me," said Penhaligon. "And then I'll unlock the portcullis gate for you."

"Sounds dangerous, Penhaligon," said Hotchi. "What if ye gets caught?"

Penhaligon shrugged. "What other choice do we have?"

The loch was ice-cold. Penhaligon sat between the dorsal fins on the serpent's neck as they glided across the steely sheet of water with barely a ripple. His heart beat loudly. He was not sure what lay ahead. All he knew was that he must not fail. He must rescue the golden egg.

As they approached the portcullis, the serpent began to sink beneath the water. It was pitch-black and silent as death as they swam through a long tunnel. Penhaligon held his breath. Did the serpent know that he could not breathe underwater and that soon he would run out of air? Water rushed past his head in a stream of bubbles as they continued forward.

Still they did not rise to the surface.

Penhaligon felt the first grip of panic. He must hold on for a little longer. Just when he thought he could not hold his breath for a minute more, a sudden peace flowed through him. He knew then that the serpent understood his fears. Finally, she rose toward a light and they burst through the surface, Penhaligon gulping at the air. They were in some kind of boathouse below the castle. There were the two rowboats, tied to a small landing. Fishing tackle lay in a heap against the wall. Close to one of the boats was Sir Derek's matching slipper.

Penhaligon climbed the steps to the landing and shook himself dry as best he could. He waved to the serpent as she disappeared beneath the water. He jumped into one of the boats and rowed back along the tunnel to the portcullis.

A rusty wheel was attached to the side of the gate. He had to use all his strength to turn the wheel just an inch. After that, no matter how hard he tried, the wheel would not budge. He realized that the gate was padlocked. He had no means of breaking the lock open. He was on his own unless he could find another way to let the others in.

After rowing back to the landing, he tiptoed up the steps leading from the boathouse. He was hoping that Dredge would not have bothered placing sentries, and so far he was in luck.

The narrow steps led into a hallway. Which way should he turn? He could smell fish cooking. Where there was a kitchen, there was usually a door to the outside. He turned toward the smell and passed by a dining hall. Looking inside, he was startled to see dozens of sleeping ferrets, some with their heads down on the table, others in a snoring heap. At least I'm in the right place, thought Penhaligon.

He stole farther along the hallway. The fish smelled delicious, and his mouth was watering. He reached the kitchen and peeked around the open door. A fire was burning in a grate, its flames reflected in the polished copper pans that hung around the hearth. No one was there that he could see, but on the kitchen table was a platter of freshly cooked fish, still steaming.

Penhaligon's snout twitched and he took one step toward the table just to look when a voice behind him said: "I'd recognize those ugly big ears and straggly brush anywhere."

Penhaligon whipped around to see Sir Derek standing behind him. The cat had a sword pointed at Penhaligon.

"Hello, Sir Derek. Nice place you have here."

"I don't actually remember inviting you in, Penhaligon. Oh, sorry, I heard it was *Sir* Penhaligon these days." Derek tsked and smoothed his waxed whiskers.

"It's all right; you can call me Penhaligon," said Penhaligon.

"What are you doing here?"

"I have come to collect something that Dredge

stole, a golden egg. It is very important. Many lives are at stake."

"Oh, another mission of kindness and virtue, eh? It's a wonder they don't call you Saint Penhaligon," said Derek with a sneer.

"I just want the egg. Where is it?"

"What makes you think I would help you, of all creatures? You had me locked up in Tamar's damp and smelly dungeon for months, and then I suffered terrible humiliation at the hands of . . . of . . . that lot." He gestured behind him toward the snoring pile of ferrets.

"You put yourself in the dungeon, Sir Derek, with your greed and cruelty."

"Bah! Well, now it's your turn. I'm sure Dredge will be very happy to see you." He turned to call the ferrets.

"Wait!" Penhaligon's mind was racing. He had to think. How could he make a deal? There had to be something he could offer. . . . "Sir Derek, if you help me, I promise you great reward."

Derek turned around. "Great reward, eh? What could a country-bumpkin fox like you possibly give me?"

Penhaligon decided that being honest was the best

place to start. "The truth is I need the egg to make a cure for *febra lupi,* wolf fever. The disease has learned how to jump from one creature to another."

The fox was surprised to see that he suddenly had Derek's complete attention. "It's spreading quickly," he continued. "If we can't make a cure, many will die. It's very contagious."

Sir Derek's sword dropped to his side. "What are the symptoms?" he asked in a hoarse whisper.

"Well, first a fever."

Derek's sword dropped to the floor with a clatter. "Oh my," he said, hand to his forehead. "I think my servant had it. He's from *the local village.*" Derek spoke the words as though they left a bad taste in his mouth.

Penhaligon Brush, being a gentleman fox, would normally never have taken advantage of another's misfortunate misunderstanding of the situation, but this was not a normal time.

"Flaming foxgloves!" said Penhaligon, his eyes widening with concern. "I thought you looked a lit-tle peaky. I didn't want to mention anything."

Sir Derek sat down at the table, took one look at the fish, and pushed the platter away.

"Oh dear," said Penhaligon, barely able to stop

himself from smiling. "Lack of appetite is the next symptom."

Sir Derek groaned.

"And these fish do smell tasty. Shame they'll all be gone soon. Did you know the egg Dredge brought here is from a sea serpent?"

Derek nodded again. His ears had gone quite flat.

"Did you also know," continued Penhaligon, "that sea serpents eat their own weight in fish every week?"

Derek groaned again.

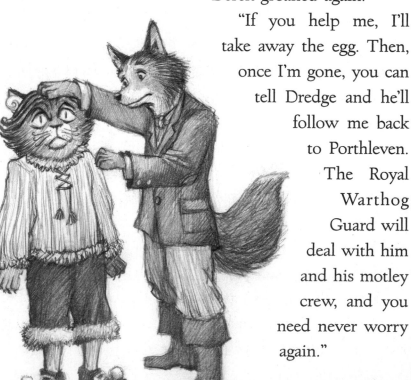

"If you help me, I'll take away the egg. Then, once I'm gone, you can tell Dredge and he'll follow me back to Porthleven. The Royal Warthog Guard will deal with him and his motley crew, and you need never worry again."

Sir Derek looked at Penhaligon from under half-closed eyelids.

"Feeling tired?" asked Penhaligon. "Hmm, you may be more advanced than I thought. May I feel your ears?"

Sir Derek, meek as a kitten, leaned his head toward Penhaligon's outstretched paw. The fox gently examined the cat's ears: "Hmm . . . oh dear . . . I thought as much." Then Penhaligon finally announced, "We'd better hurry so that I can get the remedy to you as soon as possible. Now, where did you say the egg was?"

Penhaligon followed Derek up the winding stairs to the first floor. They padded down a long hallway hung with tapestries and lined with empty suits of armor clasping a variety of ancient weapons. When they came to a circular tower at the end of the hall, they followed another winding stair upward until Sir Derek stopped outside a wooden door.

"The egg is in there—with Dredge. I cannot help you anymore. I need to lie down."

Penhaligon nodded. "I promise to send the cure for your illness as soon as I return safely to Porthleven, Sir Derek," said Penhaligon, hiding his grin behind his paw. The cat hurried away before Penhaligon had even opened the door. The hinges let out a squeak, and Penhaligon's stomach lurched. He stood, barely breathing, half in and half out of the room. But he heard only gentle snores coming from a bed in the corner. The room smelled strongly of ferret. He was in the right place.

A warm glow radiated from beside the bed. It was the egg, still wrapped in Elgato's velvet jacket. Dredge had not even bothered to hide it. Penhaligon had not expected it to be quite so beautiful—or quite so big. He tiptoed across to the bed and was about to pick up the egg when Dredge cried out, "No! Don't eat me! I didn't mean to steal your egg!"

Penhaligon froze before he realized Dredge was talking in his sleep. With a sigh of relief, he grasped the bundle. It was heavier than he'd expected. He got a better grip and tiptoed toward the door.

"Not so fast, matey! Guards!" shouted Dredge, and he sprang out of his bed, sword at the ready.

Penhaligon ran, the heavy egg under his arm. He reached the stairs but heard ferrets running toward him. His only escape was to follow the winding staircase upward. He climbed the steps two at a time, up and up the tower in a spiral. The egg weighed him down, and Dredge was gaining fast.

"You've nowhere to go, Penhaligon Brush!" screamed the ferret. "Give me my egg!"

"Never!" shouted Penhaligon as he struggled onward. He burst through a door at the top and found himself outside, on the roof of a turreted tower. He was cold, he was exhausted—and he was trapped.

Dredge appeared at the doorway. A gang of ugly looking ferrets, swords drawn, stood behind him.

"Give me the egg, Penhaligon. Make it easy on yourself. You've nowhere to go. Give me the egg, and maybe I'll let you live." Dredge took one step toward him.

Penhaligon backed up against a cold stone turret. It was true: he had nowhere to go except over the edge and down to the rocks and the loch below.

"You'll let me live?" he said bitterly. "Why would I want to live when all those around me are dying? You don't know the value of this egg. I need this eggshell, Dredge, to make the cure for *febra lupi*. The fever can jump species now. All the young ones are sick. Can't you find it in your heart to do the right thing?"

Dredge sneered. "You would crack the egg, Mr. Do-the-right-thing? You may save your pathetic friends and family, but when you break the egg, you will kill the serpent inside. You are no better than I, Penhaligon. We both want the egg for our own purposes. Now give it

to me and maybe I'll consider selling you the shell after it has hatched." He took another step closer.

Penhaligon looked over the ramparts behind him and climbed onto the wall. He closed his eyes. "Come one step further, Dredge, and I'll jump. Then no one will have the egg."

"You haven't got the nerve," growled Dredge. "Both you and the egg will be scrambled."

"Then scrambled I will be," said Penhaligon. He leaped, with the egg, into the darkness.

D redge stared in disbelief. "My egg!" he roared, and ran over to the ramparts. "I can't believe he did that!" He frantically searched the darkness below. He saw a flash of silver. Then he heard a laugh . . . Penhaligon's laugh.

"Sorry, Dredge. I couldn't resist one last trick!" Penhaligon appeared in front of him as if floating in midair.

Dredge could not believe his beady eyes: "What the . . . !" As Penhaligon floated even higher, Dredge saw that the fox was standing atop the serpent's head. Furious, he swung his sword at the stone ramparts, showering his ferrets with a hail of angry sparks. "Get down there on the double and CATCH him!" he screamed.

The ferrets tumbled down the steps, eager to escape the wrath of their leader.

"Come back here and fight, you coward!" Dredge yelled at Penhaligon.

"Sorry, Dredge. I have to go and 'do the right thing,' remember?" The fox jumped down onto the serpent's neck, between the dorsal fins. "Back to Hotchi's boat," he told the serpent.

But in her hurry to reach the water, she snaked her neck a little too quickly, causing Penhaligon to slide from between her dorsal fins. And the egg bundle slipped from his grasp. He threw out an arm and just managed to grab a sleeve of Elgato's coat. He pulled the heavy egg toward him while trying to stay astride the squirming neck. The knot in the smooth, soft velvet sleeves was slowly coming undone. The egg's sling was breaking and there was nothing he could do. And then all he was holding was an empty jacket. The egg seemed to float in the air for a second before falling, falling, falling—down toward the rocks.

"No!" he cried. His howls echoed over the lonely loch.

The serpent looped and coiled, trying to catch the egg in her mouth, but she could not. There was a resounding crack as the egg bounced off a rock, fell into the loch, and sank from view.

Then there was silence.

No one moved.

The serpent let out a wail loud enough to wake the souls of those dead for a thousand seasons.

Penhaligon's quest was at an end.

No more hard choices needed to be made; they had all been made for him.

But then Penhaligon heard another wail. It was a much tinier wail, coming from the water. He quickly scanned the loch's surface. There, bobbing up and down, was the small head of a hatchling serpent. It looked a bit odd. Penhaligon squinted his eyes. "Flaming foxgloves!" he cried. For there was not just one baby serpent's head; there were *two* baby serpents' heads!

The mother serpent hit the water with a splash. Penhaligon held on tight as she snaked toward her new babies. "Watch out!" he shouted, spying Dredge's bow ferrets rowing from the open portcullis. The serpent hissed in anger.

On board Hotchi's boat, the hedgehog realized that the hatchlings' fate was in his paws. "Raise the anchor! We 'ave to save them baby serpents!" he cried as he scurried to raise the sails.

By now Dredge had made it down to the boat-house. He rowed his boat with the power of six ferrets, screaming at the top of his lungs, "I'll reward the ferrets who capture those serpents . . . and who kill that fox!"

The bow ferrets stood in their rickety boat, arrows aimed at Penhaligon.

"Fire!" ordered their captain.

A hail of arrows flew toward Penhaligon. The serpent dove under the water just in time, almost washing her passenger from her back. When they surfaced, Dredge was almost upon the hatchlings. The mother roared in anger and streaked toward his rowboat. Penhaligon hung on for dear life. She swam around Dredge's boat as he slashed at her with his sword.

"Shoot the serpent!" he ordered his ferrets.

Hotchi had sailed as close to the squeaking hatchlings as he dared in the choppy water.

"How we get the leetle things?" cried Elgato.

"Lower me over the side," said Pig-wiggy. "I'll grab 'em."

The serpent swam faster and faster around Dredge's boat, and soon it was caught up in a circle of current. He held on to the sides of his rocking rowboat to steady himself.

"Shoot! I order you!" he yelled again.

But the bow ferrets' arrows simply flew past the serpent, who was a target that moved way too fast.

Penhaligon felt dizzy, but if he let go, he'd be a sitting duck in the water. He would have to hold on for this wild ride as long as he could.

Meanwhile, the fishing boat bobbed up and down erratically, making it difficult for Hotchi and Elgato to stand as they dangled Pig-wiggy over the side.

"Grab 'em," cried Hotchi.

The guinea pig tried to scoop up the hatchlings, but they swam away in fear.

Still the serpent circled around and around Dredge's boat in a frenzy. So strong was the circular current that a

depression started to form in the center. The dip grew deeper and deeper until a huge whirlpool was formed. Dredge clung to his boat as it skimmed the edges.

Pig-wiggy had managed to grab one of the hatchlings by the tail and tuck it inside his shirt. The bow ferrets were almost upon them.

"Quick, Mister 'Otchi, cast your net!" shouted Elgato. And while the cat held on to Pig-wiggy for dear life, Hotchi cast his fishing net over the approaching ferrets' boat. Tails and snouts were tangled in the mesh. The ferrets shouted angrily. It gave Pig-wiggy just enough time to grab the second hatchling.

"Pull us up!" he yelled.

Penhaligon watched in amazement as mud and huge old tree branches were churned up from the bottom of the loch, and something else—something shiny—the halves of the golden eggshell! He made a grab for them.

But Dredge had spotted the shell halves too. "Oh no you don't, Penhaligon Brush!" he shouted, his boat still spinning with the current. "This is *my* fortune."

The bow ferrets' boat was now also caught in the whirlpool, and they, Dredge, and the serpent chased each other as if they were on some ridiculous merry-go-round.

Penhaligon reached again for a piece of the shell, but then it was gone, spiraling around the bubbling cone.

Dredge leaned so far over the edge of his boat that his weight tipped it dangerously to the edge of the whirlpool while the terrified bow ferrets held on, unable to do anything except howl in fear as they stared into the murky depths that threatened to swallow them.

Desperate, Penhaligon stretched his arms as far as he could, ready for when the shell halves bobbed around again. The village young ones were counting on him. He must not fail.

But then he heard a gleeful screech. Looking over, he saw Dredge with half of the golden shell in his paws. Penhaligon's heart sank, but then the other half swirled toward him. With hope restored, Penhaligon reached out as it spun by him again. He touched it—

And then the game was won.

"Got it!" yelled Dredge. "Yes, yes, yes! It's mine . . . all mine!"

It was over. Dredge had both golden halves. Penhaligon's spirit was as broken as the pieces of shell that Dredge held triumphantly in his dirty paws.

"Ha! Penhaligon Brush, you lose!" Dredge hugged

the eggshells to his body, laughing wildly. "I'm rich! I'm rich!" he cried. His boat rocked from side to side as he jiggled around.

"Flaming foxgloves!" shouted Penhaligon. "Watch out!"

Dredge's rowboat suddenly pitched to the side and the ferret was flung into the center of the whirlpool. Penhaligon watched in horror as Dredge, still laughing his hideous laugh, was sucked down, still clutching the shells. "Mine . . . all mine!" he screeched just before he disappeared from view.

The serpent stopped swimming. Slowly, the loch became smooth and glassy. In the dawn's light, there was barely a trace of the turmoil that had just taken place—just a couple of twigs floating in a forgotten current.

Desperate, Penhaligon pictured the golden shell halves and frantically hummed the lullaby. "I must find that shell!" he cried.

The serpent dutifully dove under the water, carrying Penhaligon down to the bottom of the loch. The floor of the loch was freezing and pitch-black as they zigzagged across it. Penhaligon knew that she would find the pieces of her eggshell . . . if they were there. They found nothing.

She rose to the surface to allow Penhaligon to take a breath and then dove again, this time darting in a different direction. She swam close to the steep side of the loch, hesitating for a moment. Had she seen something? Penhaligon could see almost nothing in the murky water, but then he caught a movement out the corner of his eye. He turned, but it was just the waving weed clinging to the sides of the loch. There was no trace of Dredge or the golden shell.

The hatchlings appeared in Penhaligon's thoughts. The new mother was anxious. He patted her sides. Let's go up, he thought, and so she spiraled up to Hotchi's boat, where Penhaligon slipped off her back and onto the deck, exhausted.

Elgato and Pig-wiggy placed the squeaking hatchlings onto their mother's back. She gave a triumphant roar and sank beneath the dark waters.

The bow ferrets, like their leader, had vanished.

ໃ ໃ ໃ ໃ

No one had much to say on the trip back to Porthleven. Rowan's words haunted Penhaligon: "There is no cure for wolf fever." He stood alone at the stern of Hotchi's boat. The lullaby entered his head and he hummed it gently to himself . . . it soothed breaking hearts, Rowan had said. But Penhaligon's heart wasn't just breaking; it was shattered.

🔔 🔔 🔔 🔔

The blaze of pink rhododendrons had faded. Penhaligon trudged up the driveway, thankful that there was no sign of the guard. He could barely bring himself to enter Ferball Manor Hospital; was it already too late for Donald?

Gertrude and Hannah Hotchi-witchi were on the ward. It was the first time Penhaligon had seen the many sick young creatures. His paws suddenly felt cold and clammy.

"Penhaligon," said Gertrude, "we're so glad to see you."

Penhaligon made anxiously for Donald's bed, but a sorry young badger lay there instead. The badger's little claws gripped the blanket as he looked with frightened eyes at the travel-worn fox. Penhaligon's head spun, and he felt as though the blood had drained from his body in one gush.

"Donald?" he whispered.

"He was very ill. We moved him upstairs to Rowan's room."

"You mean he's still alive?"

"Well . . . yes. Penhaligon, I made the cure as you said, but it doesn't seem to have made much difference. Dora is much improved, though. And I think maybe some of the other young ones are feeling better—"

Penhaligon interrupted her: "How is Rowan?"

Gertrude shook her head and wiped her brow with her apron. Penhaligon didn't wait for her answer, but took the stairs two at a time. He bounded through the door of the bedroom.

Rowan and Donald looked small, huddled together in the great bed. The fire was burning cheerily in the grate, and the sun was beaming through the large bay window. The acrid smell of bog-mud poultice was strong. Gertrude arrived with a small bowl.

"I've made a new batch, Penhaligon—with the stony lunacrop, just like you said. I checked the ingredients twice. Donald seems more comfortable, but he's shown no signs of improvement."

"No," said Penhaligon. "The cure will not work without the serpent shell, and that's gone forever." He sat by Rowan's side and held her paw.

Gertrude began to cry softly. "Shall I give this to him, then?" She held out the bowl.

"I'll do it, Gertrude." Penhaligon moved to Donald's

side of the bed. "Here, Donald." He coaxed the cub, holding a spoon. The cub stared with glazed eyes. "I want to tell you of all the strange and wonderful things I've seen while I've been away. And you'll never guess who I bumped into. . . . Remember that stinky ferret Captain Dredge? Well, what a surprise that was! Donald, can you hear me?"

But the cub's eyes closed and his head flopped to one side.

"Donald?" said Penhaligon. "Don't give up. We must go to Howling Island to meet your grandfather. He's a chief of the Romany wolves. The trees are so tall, and there are a thousand stars that grow on top of a mountain. Donald? Donald!"

Large tears rolled down Penhaligon's snout, dropping into the bowl of useless medicine. Should he have kept the cure in the silver flask for Donald? But how could he have left Dora to suffer her fate? It wasn't fair: one fox shouldn't have to make so many choices.

Bah! Penhaligon realized that his tears had dripped into the bowl. He pulled out his handkerchief from his pocket. A silver scale fell to the floor, flashing in the sunlight. It was the scale that had come loose so long ago as he tended the serpent on the Gassaro Sea.

He picked it up and stared. "I wonder," he said,

almost to himself. Well, it was worth a try. "Gertrude, give me the mortar and pestle—quickly, please."

The scale crumbled easily with the pounding pestle, and he stirred the silver flakes into the fresh cure. Penhaligon tipped three spoonfuls into Donald's open mouth. He had no idea if this was too little or too much.

Gertrude took the bowl gently from his paws and spoon-fed Rowan the same mixture.

Then Penhaligon laid his head on the bed and closed his weary eyes. He hoped that Bancroft and Mawgan were right—that there was no such thing as coincidence. He prayed that the silver scale had fallen out of his pocket at that moment for a reason.

🕯 🕯 🕯 🕯

The fire was out when Penhaligon heard a weak voice calling him.

"Penhaligon! Wake up."

"Flaming foxgloves, how could I have fallen asleep?" He turned to see Rowan watching him. Her eyes were clear, her nose wet and shiny.

"Rowan!" He felt her ears. The fever was cooling.

Rowan managed a smile. "Well . . . it's about time you came back from your gallivanting!" she scolded.

Penhaligon was speechless. He studied Donald's face, expecting the worst. But the cub lay quietly sleeping. He was breathing without the noisy rattle of a cough, and his nose was also damp. Penhaligon could hardly believe his eyes. The cure had worked, without the golden shell!

"Bancroft! Gertrude!" he shouted. "Come quick!"

🕯 🕯 🕯 🕯

Bancroft had made up a fire. Penhaligon sat beside Rowan as she sipped her nettle tea. Donald was curled up next to her, uttering little snores.

The fox took a bite of some delicious turnip cake that had been delivered along with the dozens of food baskets left on the Ferball Manor doorstep. The largest basket had been from the Stoat family, whose young one, along with Cedric C. Otter, was one of the first to go home. For it had been as Rowan had expected:

the disease had taken a different form in the non-wolves. The stony lunacrop cure that Gertrude had first prepared was enough to cure their illness.

Rowan placed her tea on the bedside table. "Don't think you're leaving me behind next time, Penhaligon. I've had to do all the hard work while you were away, and besides that, I nearly fell off a cliff. Oh yes, and you'll have to buy me a new pair of britches for when you take it into your head to have another adventure. Look at mine—they are completely ruined, and . . ."

Penhaligon planted a kiss on Rowan's nose. "Rest now, Mrs. Mud Monster. I'll never leave you again. And to be honest, I think I've had enough adventure."

Rowan rolled her eyes. "That's what you said last time."

Epilogue

After the Porthleven quarantine was lifted, Crown Prince Tamar and Princess Katrina arrived to help celebrate the newly rescheduled Ferball Festival. The sun shone down, and young creatures squealed in delight as Penhaligon led the parade through the village, dressed in his slimy seaweed Sea Witch costume. Old Amon had indeed done him proud, and oddly, the fresh, fishy seaweed smell somehow made Penhaligon feel lucky to be alive.

The fiddlers and drummers played a merry jig, with Donald and Dora heading the dancers in their blue-and-scarlet costumes. Dora did not trip Donald even once.

Farmer and Mrs. Pigswiggin proudly took third place out of the three couples that entered the duet-singing contest, and Gertrude and Rowan had to cover their smirks when Penhaligon awarded the prize for Best Cottage in Bloom to Mrs. Goat.

"Thank goodness for that," bleated Bill Goat. "Maybe now we can concentrate on feeding me instead of the flowers."

Elgato Furrari and Hotchi had become firm friends, and the silver-gray cat promised to visit Porthleven often, especially as he decided that the cowslip ale at the Cat and Fiddle was far superior to that of the Warped Board Public House in Falmouth. Rowan, as a thank-you, had given him her silver serpent's scales so he could fix up the *Jagged Claw*, as he never did see his gold. The proud ship now lay at anchor off Brigand's Point, looking as fine as any royal Spatavian clipper, and with his new velvet jacket and sleekly groomed fur, Elgato was indeed a handsome figure.

Pig-wiggy's dream came true when Elgato offered him a job as first mate. He was the happiest guinea pig around, especially after using Penhaligon's walnut-oil salve on his ginger Mohawk. It was never patchy again.

Penhaligon took his time before sending a messenger with Sir Derek's "cure," which actually was no more than ginger compote and honey. Sir Derek was happy to send Menhenin's precious book that Dredge had left back to Porthleven, as he would rather not have anything to do with wolves or sea serpents, thank you very much.

The serpent returned to Howling Island to raise her hatchlings, but as soon as they were old enough, the family made visits back to the Ferball Manor dungeon, carrying messages between Penhaligon and his father. Mawgan was to visit just as soon as Elgato could fetch him, he said.

The cubs were so excited to learn about Mawgan that they begged Bancroft to help them study Menhenin's book so they could learn about Romany wolves. Bancroft had never seen them so enthusiastic about learning.

The hatchlings spent much time in the sea by Ferball Manor. Donald and Dora took them for long swims, shined their silver scales, and planted stony lunacrop in the gardens to keep them happy and healthy. They also taught them all sorts of mischievous tricks and were constantly in trouble for scaring the villagers and swimming too fast.

As for Captain Dredge, he was never seen again, although Sir Derek swore that on moonlit nights

he heard an eerie howl onthe windy loch, crying,
"Mine . . . all mine!"

No one knew for sure why the Curse had
returned, but thanks to Penhaligon and his intrepid
friends never again did any creature live in fear of
the Curse of the Romany Wolves.